SPIRIT OF THE HIGHWAY

THE HIGHWAY TRILOGY
PART II

DEBORAH SWIFT

Copyright © 2015 by Deborah Swift.

All rights reserved. No part of this publication may be reproduced, distributed or transmitted in any form or by any means, including photocopying, recording, or other electronic or mechanical methods, without the prior written permission of the author, except in the case of brief quotations embodied in critical reviews and certain other noncommercial uses permitted by copyright law.
For permission requests, contact the author www.deborahswift.com

This is a work of fiction. Names, characters, places, and incidents are a product of the author's imagination. Locales and public names are sometimes used for atmospheric purposes. Any resemblance to actual people, living or dead, or to businesses, companies, events, institutions, or locales is completely coincidental.

Book Layout ©2013 BookDesignTemplates.com

Spirit of the Highway/Deborah Swift -- 1st ed.
ISBN 978-1517279486

ALSO BY DEBORAH SWIFT

The Lady's Slipper
The Gilded Lily
A Divided Inheritance

Teen fiction
Shadow on the Highway
Spirit of the Highway

PRAISE FOR DEBORAH SWIFT

"there is no greater compliment than, 'Give me more!'"
Susanna Gregory

'her characters are so real they linger in the mind long after the book is back on the shelf'

The Historical Novels Review

And where is your soft bed of down, my love?
And where is your white Holland sheet?
And where the fair maid who watches over you
As you take your long, sightless sleep?

"The earth is my soft bed of down, my love,
The grass is my white Holland sheet.
And the long, hungry worms my servants
To wait on me as I sleep.

The True Lover's Ghost – traditional ballad

CHAPTER ONE

Highway to War

England, August 1651

I can hang like a mist, seep through solid walls, slither through keyholes. When you turn to look, you won't see me, just feel the chill of a frost ruffle the hairs on your neck. You will sense my presence, and stare hard into the dark, but I'll be already gone, into a past or future where you can't follow.

My sister Abigail likes to tell my story, but she often gets it wrong. Sometimes she doesn't understand, being deaf and all. Besides, she only ever tells her side of the tale, and not how easy it is for simple events to shift and change and be embroidered into a legend. That's because, like the rest of the living, she can't have my perspective.

Being dead has its disadvantages. I feel nothing, not the grit underfoot, not the weave of the linen shirt on my body. I will never feel those coarse things again, only the subtlest tingle as I move through the trees, through objects more compressed than I am myself. The solid part of me is my feelings, and they haven't diminished. Sometimes I'm all anguish, sometimes a wisp of temper, or a vapour of tenderness. And I can look back on myself, the living me, and wish it had been different. Yes, sometimes I'm a cloud of regret.

The day I went to war I didn't look back, despite the fact I could feel Kate's eyes on my neck all the way down the highway. Or maybe because of it. I fixed my gaze on the ranks of marching men, not wanting to let Kate see how much I cared. How heavy the soldiers' footfalls seem now! Though Kate was left behind, her face seemed to burn before me, her expression troubled, her green eyes full of questions and doubt about me going to war.

We would win, I thought to myself, and the King's scurvy men had to fall. I was angry inside for feeling so much, so I gripped my musket tighter to my shoulder. Pray God the rumours were right and our numbers would be greater than theirs, because I had to survive. If I did not, my Kate would be left to the Fanshawes, and that I couldn't bear.

I marched on. Though when I say marching, it was more of a slouching, a rousing of dust as the rabble clanked their disorderly way down the road, their provision pots banging against their pikes and muskets. I can hardly remember the smell of that dust now, nor the heat of the sun, nor the grit on my kerchief as I wiped my wet cheeks.

It was sweat, I told myself; that's why my eyes were watering so.

'You at Marston Moor?' A shorter man appeared at my shoulder and fell in next to me. His face was flat and open, and blue with old bruises.

'No. I just joined.' It was a relief to speak.

'So late?'

I bridled at his slight reproof. 'I don't hold with armies.'

'Then why'd you join?' He pushed his lank, black fringe out of his eyes and fixed me with an owl-like look.

'To finish it. To make a new world, where the men who work are masters of their own lives. So womenfolk can rest safe again in their own beds.'

'Ah. A girl is it?'

I sniffed, hitched my musket further onto my shoulder. 'Don't you want to change the world?'

'Me? Nah, just want to survive it.'

We marched on in silence except for the sound of tramping boots. The first cold vestiges of fear had begun to worm their way into my blood.

My short companion glanced over to me, 'Odds are for us, they say. We'll whip them this time.' He grinned, showing a gap the width of my little finger between his front teeth. 'That whelp of a King won't know what's hit him.'

I nodded, tried to look more knowledgeable than I felt. Father was just ahead of me somewhere, on his horse, leading the line. At the thought of him I clenched my teeth, marched faster. The drunken bastard. I wondered how I could ever have admired him.

'Hey, slow down, don't want to wear yourself out, do you?' The short man quickened to stay abreast of me. 'I'm Cuthbert Briggs, by the way. Folks call me Cutch.'

'Ralph,' I said.

'You a farmer? Thought so. From your hands, see. Harvester's scratches, no mistaking them. I was apprenticed to a wheelwright, before all this. Can't remember a thing about it now, been all over the country this last five years. Look.' He rolled up a sleeve, pointed to a livid purple scar. 'Sword cut. But I slit the devil's throat in return.' He laughed. 'You stick with me, you'll be right. I can mend anything, me. I've learnt bone-setting, amputation, all manner of surgeon's skills. Let's hope we don't need 'em, eh?'

I thanked him, but knew I'd rather be alone. The air was charged with excitement, with the buzzing, anxious thoughts of men intent on battle. Some of us would die, it was certain, and nobody wanted to be that man.

Moisture gathered on my upper lip, but I licked it away, concentrated on the buff-coloured back of the marching man in front. If we won, *when* we won, and Cromwell was victorious, then what would happen to Kate? My stomach lurched.

That's what came of falling in love with a Royalist. Someone on the wrong bloody side.

I thanked God our troops were well away from Markyate Manor. For now, at least, Kate would be safe.

My feet were all-over blistered. Four days it took, to cover the hundred miles, until we saw the pitched towers of the cathedral and the city ramparts shimmering ahead of us, pink in the heat. I stared at their bulk. There would be young women like Kate behind those walls, afraid of men like me.

Cutch threw down his backpack on the verge and pulled off his helmet to reveal a thatch of damp black hair. I joined him whilst we waited for orders.

We shared a rough knob of bread and an apple that Cutch boasted he'd robbed from an orchard the day before.

A couple of tired-looking women, camp followers, sat down next to us, with hopeful expressions. Shaking my head, I tore my bread in two and handed a lump to the nearest woman, the one with the yellow hair. She crammed the crust between her teeth, swallowed, then wordlessly uncorked a flagon of small beer and handed it over.

I took a swig but had been sitting only a few moments when a horseman appeared, looking up and down the lolling men. They stood to attention as he passed. I prepared to stand too, but as the man got closer I saw it was Father. I stayed where I was.

Cutch rose straight away, and dipped his head as Father drew up in front of us and reined his horse to a stop. Father slid down and landed heavily with a jangle of spurs and sword.

'Ah, Cutch,' he said, handing him the reins. He turned to me, 'Mind you stick with Briggs here. He's a seasoned soldier. They say we shouldn't have much trouble judging by the terrain. We've got them cornered. Rats in a nest, they are. And the Welsh supporters have given the young King the old heave-ho. But watch your back, son, because there's still a bunch of Scots waiting to give us a thrashing.' He paused, tried to look me in the eyes, but I kept my gaze firmly on the point where the tip of my boot met the ground.

Father cleared his throat, rubbed his sandy beard, then squatted to crouch next to me, out of the women's earshot. 'Ralph lad. I wanted to wish you…well, to wish you luck.' He reached out a hand to clap me on the shoulder but I shrugged away.

'I know you're still smarting from what happened at Markyate Manor,' Father said, 'but these things happen in war.'

'You were going to rape a woman, Father.' I spoke the words with icy coolness, loud enough to shame him. 'A girl who had done nothing wrong, except to be in her own home. In our own village. She could have been your own daughter.'

'She's a Royalist,' he said, standing up. 'She spat on us often enough. Her family taxed us to death and well you know it.'

'It's no excuse. I saw you. It was not done in anger. You were laughing, drunk. You were taunting her for entertainment. It is that I can't forgive.' I turned away. I caught a glimpse of the yellow-haired girl, her wide-open eyes showing she had heard every word. She stood, made a 'V' gesture at Father, and stalked off.

'What's the fuss? We let her go didn't we?' Father's face had turned the colour of a plum.

'Only because I was there to stop you.' I closed my eyes to shut out the image of what I had seen, Kate's kicking and struggling to escape. 'How many more, Father? How many other young girls have you terrorized whilst poor Mother sits at home fretting over your fate?'

He dropped his gaze.

There was my answer. I felt sick. Ashamed to be his son.

Father climbed awkwardly back onto his horse, exchanging a look with Cutch, who nodded back to him. 'You don't understand.' Father sighed as he took up the reins. 'You will. When you've seen action.'

I watched him gallop away. My belly was sore with a pain deep inside. I used to be so proud of my father, of his swaggering strength, of his assertive way of talking. I used to look up to him with a mixture of awe and terror. But now I was taller than he, and suddenly he seemed empty, as if I'd been admiring a man of straw. I slumped back down to the ground.

Cutch dropped his backside down next to me. 'Women. They're a curse. He's a fine man, your father. You should show him more respect. He's saved many a man through his courage. I'd not be here today if it wasn't for him.'

I ignored Cutch, until a sergeant came to divide us up. Some men to the River Severn and some to the Teme, to make pontoon bridges across the river. I asked another soldier why, and he told me most of the bridges had been destroyed by the King's troops. All except the one at the main gate, and the Royalist Scots were thick as butter all over it.

I pushed away from Cutch into the group for the Teme, but at the last minute he broke ranks and joined me. The sergeant couldn't be bothered to complain, but merely looked annoyed and gestured to Cutch to hurry.

'Nearly lost you then, friend,' Cutch said.

I gave him a thin smile.

That night we had to drag all the boats on the river together and tie them to each other to make a wooden crossing. It was a relief to be doing something, though the water was deep and slopped up to my waist. Cutch and I hauled the first skiffs from the shore and tied them together. All along the bank the glint of breastplates as other men scurried furtively to drag more row-boats into position. There was not a fisherman in sight, the rumour of our troops had gone before us, and all sensible anglers had fled. Only the cows lowed plaintively in the fields and a night time owl screeched her warning.

Across the river it was a dark mouth of blackness. Somewhere over there would be men like us, chafing, their stomachs watery with fear, dreading the morrow but willing it to come quickly, unable to sleep.

'Sssh!' Cutch put a hand on my shoulder, and I nearly leapt out of my breeches. It was hard to be quiet. I had to rip the planks from the fences, whilst other men splintered the farmer's cart with swords and knives and brute strength. Finally we managed to fasten the wood into a serviceable walkway. Our foreheads dripped with sweat, but the pontoon bridge on our side swayed on the undulating surface of the river. I wish I had known then it was a bridge to hell.

CHAPTER TWO

Pike and Musket

I'd hardly slept. The distant whinnies of the enemy's nervous horses set me on edge. When they fell silent just before the dawn, and a faint rustling betrayed an army on the move, I could bear it no longer. I buckled on the breastplate they'd issued me with, and fished in my bag for the powder flask and pouch of lead shot.

As I pulled them out, a scrap of white dropped to the grass. I reached down to retrieve it. Kate's handkerchief. I'd unthinkingly put it in my bag after I'd dried her parting tears. The flimsy linen was so fragile, with its embroidered monogram of 'K. F.', the tiny stitches of the *fleurs de lis* of the Fanshawe crest. I brought it to my nose, inhaled as if to smell her. The thought of her pale translucent skin, her copper hair, made a chasm in my chest.

From the corner of my eye I saw Cutch watching me through half-open eyes. I hurriedly turned my back, pushed the handkerchief deep inside my jerkin next to my heart.

'They're on the move,' Cutch whispered.

On my right-hand side pikes bristled to upright, an instant thicket of trees. The sight of their pointed metal ends made me even more apprehensive. Father would be riding amongst them, in breastplate and helmet, barking out his orders. Pray God he was sober enough. I was momentarily sorry for those men.

I heaved the musket onto my shoulder not a moment too soon. The order 'Cast about!' came in a whisper, passed from man to man. No doubt the sergeant hoped to conceal our existence from the enemy as long as possible. A sudden movement to my right and the forest of pikes made for the pontoon in an ungainly stagger. The make-shift bridge had been finished from the other side, but it wobbled and drifted and several men fell into the river, unable to stay upright with the weight of their pikes.

'Poor bastards,' Cutch said, next to me, jamming on his helmet.

The second wave of pikes was across when a rumbling noise turned my throat dry. On my left flank the Scots cavalry exploded into view, not head-on as we'd expected, but from the side.

'Where the hell did they come from?' Cutch shouted.

I'd no time to wonder, because our musketeers began to stream across the field to block their path. Fearful of being left behind, I stumbled after them until they threw themselves down to their bellies in the wet dew.

'Place the Charge!' Yates, the artillery sergeant, sounded calm.

Be still. I willed my hands to stop shaking, as I planted the stock of the gun on the parched ground and tipped powder down its muzzle. Damn. Half of it fell over my boot, but I fished out a musket ball just the same and dropped it down on top.

'Wadding!'

My fumbling fingers found the small pieces of shredded cloth, but my eyes were fixed on the cavalry who were galloping full tilt at Father's pikemen who formed the wall between us and those sharp hooves. I saw father dismount and order his ranks into a bristling hedge.

'Ram it down!'

Panicking, I thrust my scouring stick down the barrel until the wadding was compacted on top of the ball.

Why hadn't I practiced this more when Father told me to?

'Prepare to give fire!'

Lord have mercy. I dived to the ground, but my eyes were chained to the scene in front. Ahead of me a pike-man crumpled beneath the charging horses, his pike splintering like a matchstick, his body soon lost under the dust of the pounding hooves.

I sucked in my breath, jammed the cord in the serpent jaws of my musket. A small boy ran up and held out a burning coal. At first I didn't understand. A boy? Here? But he pressed the coal to my cord, and then I understood. It was shaking about so much that the cord wouldn't catch. But finally it glowed and I blew on it frantically to keep it alight.

The cavalry regrouped for a second charge.

I can do this, I told myself. I raised the butt of the gun to my shoulder and flicked open the priming pan.

'Give Fire!' The end of the order was lost in the blast.

Deafened, I dragged back the trigger and let it go.

An almighty flash. It seared my eyeballs and a kickback like a punch hit into my shoulder, forcing the breath from my lungs. I had no idea where the musket ball went, only that ahead of me horses, screaming in pain, toppled down onto the pikes, their hooves thrumming the air as if they were drowning.

I could not move, it was as if the strings to my legs were cut.

'Forward!'

Cutch and the other men lurched into action. I was pulled with them, caught in their momentum. Smoke obscured the view, but now I was actually moving, a great tide of anger bore me forwards, swamping my vision with a black haze.

I ploughed onwards, musket banging against my thigh, following Cutch's buff jerkin. He looked back for me, his face fixed in a roar, as we ran pell-mell across the field towards the pontoon bridge. Too late. Another company of enemy horses from the side. My chest felt as if it would collapse with fear. The Scots were upon us, swords glinting through the smoke in the early sun. Mouths open in a yell to urge on horses already wild-eyed with the scent of powder and blood.

'Fire!'

The artillery sergeant's order came, but I wasn't ready. It was all happening too fast. My musket was un-primed, useless. The fire from our side was sparse and erratic. The horses kept on coming.

My fingers wouldn't stop trembling. I couldn't get the powder into the barrel. Ahead of me a tall long-nosed cavalier on a chestnut horse cut down two of our company with a single swift blow. Frantically I jammed in the powder and shot. If I did not hurry, I would be next.

'Fool!' A yell in my ear. 'Fall back!' Cutch put his arm round my throat, dragged me away back towards the brake of bushes where we had been hiding. He shoved me bodily behind a hawthorn tree and rolled over, already re-loading.

'That was Edward Copthorne. Vicious devil. Don't mess with him.'

'Why? What's—'

'Prime your musket,' he said. 'You'll need it. We'll all need more cover to cross that pontoon. Talk about sitting ducks. Best stay here a while till it quietens off.'

The sounds of battle hung thick in my ears; Scots curses, men's screams, terrified squeals of horses amid gunfire and the clash of metal. I thought I did not care, but fear for my father welled up suddenly, like a spring gushes water.

'No. I'm going in again,' I said, 'my father's down there with those pikes.'

Cutch grabbed me by the arm. 'He wants you to stay out of it.'

'What do you know about it?' I tried to shake him off, but he clung on.

'I'm to watch you. He's paying me to mind you. Keep you out of trouble.'

'What?'

'He doesn't want you killed.'

'Leave go, damn you! I can look after myself.'

'Everyone needs friends in war.'

I broke away from him, started to run back down to the field where the last remaining pikemen had gathered in a knot, pikes facing outwards as they retreated before us up the bank.

As I got closer I heard my father's voice, 'Keep tight, lads!' A note of panic in his throat churned my stomach. I'd thought I didn't care anymore, but my heart knew better.

Father was on foot. There was no sign of his horse. The cavalry was re-grouping for another charge. About forty horsemen, maybe more. I counted the pikes. Twelve. The rest lay broken in the dust. Oh God. My mouth turned dry as tinder.

My gun was ready, but I knew I must use it wisely. I pulled the well-oiled trigger back on, felt for the burning match-cord hanging down. Yesterday I hated my father, now the thought of him facing those charging hooves spurred me into action.

I threw myself off to one side, knelt so that another rank of musketeers could come behind me if need be.

A movement at my shoulder and I turned to see Cutch. He exchanged a grim smile with me and settled by my side. More men lined up behind us.

A shout and the horses hung momentarily still, hooves pawing the air. Then in a single tidal bore, they charged, straight towards us.

The pikemen lowered their pikes into a bristling barrier of needles.

I twitched, about to pull the trigger, but Cutch yelled, 'Not yet! Wait for the second wave!'

My father gripped his pike, jamming it into the ground at an angle to the approaching horses. A roar of hooves. The knot of men turned into a whirlwind of dust and screaming horseflesh. My finger hovered over the trigger, but Cutch was right, the King's man dropped his flag again and the second wave of cavalry pounded towards the straggling band of pikemen.

'Now!' Cutch yelled.

I fired, but nothing happened. Shit. I'd measured wrong. The match-cord didn't reach the pan. In a panic, I fumbled to get it to the right length. Cutch's went off with a blast, and judging from the smoke and noise so did the rest. I was too late. The pikemen were running back towards us, my father stumbling amongst them, but the men on horseback cut them down, swiping their blades as they ran. I saw my father glance behind, then redouble his effort as a heavy black hunter gained on him.

Unthinking I shouldered my musket and started to run.

I sprinted till I thought my lungs would burst. The black horse was almost on top of him. I skidded to a stop. Took aim. Pulled the trigger with all my might. It exploded with an almighty thump and the man on the hunter flew up from the saddle, thudded face down in the dust.

I ran towards Father, legs struggling like underwater. From the corner of my eye I saw another chestnut horse racing straight at us; the man Cutch called Copthorne, the long-nosed cavalier. Father saw him, tripped, and in his panic had to half-crawl, half-stagger over the tussocks.

No time to re-load, but still I ran. I sensed the movement of air as the horse galloped past, clods of earth spurted up in my face as it wheeled. Copthorne's sword caught the light with a blinding arc as it swept towards my father's head. I knew before I looked that my father would be dead.

My legs would not work. I panted for breath and swayed in the dust and smoke which hung in the sudden silence.

When the air cleared, I took a few steps forward to see the field was strewn with corpses. There seemed to be only two of us left. Copthorne and I.

Copthorne threw himself off his horse and loped over to where Father lay, motionless in the dirt, and spat in his face. Then he paused over the body, lower lip trembling, until with sudden venom he stabbed his sword down into Father's chest. Another stab. And more, over and over.

'Stop!' I could not believe what I saw.

My legs were quaking so much I could barely run. As I arrived, Copthorne kicked at the body with his boot. I heard the crack of ribs. He stepped back, satisfied.

'Stop.' I hardly had a voice, but it was enough to alert him. He looked up, his eyes challenging me.

Father was lying face up. He could have been sleeping, except for the dark gash in his neck, and the fact his chest was a mass of wounds. His eyes were closed as if he could not look his enemy in the face. I stared at him a moment. Somehow it surprised me that he didn't get up to bluster and fight back.

I turned. Copthorne had strolled away and was kneeling, not more than seven or eight yards from me.

'Philip,' he called, shaking the man I'd shot, over and over as if to wake him, but the body flopped back like a fish out of water. When he stood up again, his hands were smeared with blood. He walked towards me, legs as unsteady as mine, but I drew my sword, my eyes fixed on his.

'Did you shoot that man?' he asked. His voice was too restrained, conversational, with a cut-glass edge.

I swallowed. 'Yes. He was going to cut down my father.'

'Is that your father?' He pointed with a long leather clad finger. 'George Chaplin?'

I nodded.

'Bastard. He deserved it. A thug, like all of Cromwell's vermin.' His sword hissed from its scabbard but I swung back at him before I had time to think. He was crazy. I knew that now.

'Say your prayers, then.' His blade flashed before me missing my face by a whisper.

He was taller than I, long-boned and sinewy, but I was more muscled. His sword was a long river of a blade unlike my stubby weapon. I dared not look away.

Whoosh. The air vibrated as the sharp edge whistled past my ear. I fell back, fearful to be in range. I waited for him to lift his arm high again and then rushed in underneath. With a grunt he brought his own sword down, I closed my eyes but the blow did not come. When I opened them, Cutch was fighting beside me, and his slashing blade had forced the other man back.

Another Scot came up at my shoulder, and the thick of the battle closed round us. I fought for my life, all eyes, blade whirling in front and behind. I was tiring. My arm was heavy as lead. A blast of trumpets sounded, and more thundering commotion. I faltered. Another attack from the Scots would finish me.

'It's Cromwell!' The shout was like a shot of wine fizzing through our veins.

I hacked with renewed vigour.

Cutch grabbed me by the back of my coat. 'Fall back!' he yelled, 'Make room!'

Cromwell's cavalry stormed onto the field, forcing their way through in ever greater numbers, pressing the enemy to retreat behind the city walls. Somewhere in the distance a church bell pealed, calling the faithful to prayer. Its clang sounded doleful and empty. I should pray, I thought. Father's soul needed all the prayers I could muster. But I was too exhausted to do anything but sit, panting, nauseous, head hanging dizzily between my knees.

After a while I looked up. The darkening field was strewn with mounds of colour against the green grass. Cavaliers and Roundheads side by side.
Black flies hovered in clouds around each corpse.

A shout - the order to follow, but I couldn't move. The sudden quiet was eerie. I hung back. So did Cutch. I wondered if, like me, he could not bear to leave my father lying there amidst all the broken pikes, and even more broken men. I kept glancing over to where he lay, imagining my mother and Abigail, what I could tell them. But what could I do? There was no time to bury any of our men now.

I looked for Cutch, and saw him walk over to my father's body, feel in his pockets.

'Oy!' I shouted, but he ignored me.

I stood up. Cutch was pulling father's signet ring off his finger. He slipped it into the pouch which hung at his belt.

I was about to go over, but then he left Father, went to the body of Copthorne's brother, rolled him over. He shoved something else in his pocket, started to unbuckle his scabbard.

Cutch was scavenging, and somehow this hurt more than anything else. Tears began to flow. My eyes blurred.

Cutch swaggered over, held something out on the flat of his palm. 'Look. Your father's seal.'

'Piss off. I don't want it.'

Cutch shrugged, put it in his pocket. 'I'll keep it for you. Better you should have it than anyone else. You've got to be quick to beat the professionals.'

'It feels wrong. They're not even cold yet, and you must rob them.'

'Suit yourself. But I took this for you.' He drew out a fine chased sword from the new scabbard buckled to his belt. 'From that man you shot down. You did well. He's Philip Copthorne, of Copthorne Castle. Or rather was. That's his crest.'

I ignored Cutch's pointing finger.

'Shame you didn't get his older brother too.' He stroked the chased hilt with his thumb, then held it out, 'Beautiful craftsmanship.'

I didn't want to look at it.

Cutch spat on the ground. 'Your loss. It'll be better than the one I've got. Something nice about killing the bastard aristocrats with their own weapons, wouldn't you say?'

But I had no time to answer as a blast of cannon fire from the city walls gouged a deep hole in the field only ten yards from us. Earth spattered over our shoulders like hail. 'Run!' Cutch yelled.

I followed him, stumbling, back to the brake of trees. My eyes wouldn't stop watering, washing themselves, as if they wanted to un-see what I had seen. From behind the thorn, dotted with autumn haws like beads of scarlet, I mourned the loss of my England. My father's death was unreal still, but the loss of that peaceful green field, the nature that had been sullied by such savagery; that pierced me to the bone.

CHAPTER THREE

Mercy and Vengeance

We crouched behind the cold grit parapet of Fort Royal above the Sidbury gate to the city. My shoulder was bruised and numb from the retort of my musket which I still had not the knack of using properly, and my left hand was blistered from an explosion in the pan when I'd lit the fuse, and in my panic, forgot to fire.

Now I was here, I just wanted to go home. I wanted it to be over, and to be back fishing in the lazy river, or pushing a plough. Probably that was all the Royalists wanted too. Our insistent blast of shot had sent them scurrying behind the city walls. Our men had taken the Friars Gate, and now our restless ranks of helmeted cavalry stood by. They were well-drilled, packed together, a hundred iron-clad hooves under the clank of steel and sword.

'Makes you proud, doesn't it?' Cutch said, as if to read my mind.

There was something unrelenting about the machine that was the New Model Army. I pitied those inside the city gates, the women and children dreading their order to charge. I prayed our men would be merciful, but then I'd seen what they did at Markyate Manor.

My thoughts turned again to Kate. Even here she was always with me, like a burning brand in the back of my mind. I longed for her soft womanliness, to rest my head on her shoulder, inhale her scent of cinnamon and roses.

'Penny for them?' Cutch said.

'Nothing, just thinking of home.'

'Then in God's name stop. If we're going in behind those walls, there'll be nowhere to run. Keep your wits about you and watch your back.'

'I wish it was over.'

'I wished that every day for five years,' Cutch said. 'Now I dread it.'

'Why?'

But there was no time for him to answer because the trumpet sounded and the cavalry charged forward.

In their wake, Cromwell's battle cry echoed round the fortress, 'The Lord of Hosts!' but almost immediately it was followed by our sergeant's instructions, 'Spare no souls!' he yelled.

This was it, our final push. I pelted down the narrow stone stairs, the barrel of my musket scraping on the wall, and followed the long ragged line of infantry into the city. Even from outside the walls I could hear the cathedral bells ringing their ear-splitting warning, over the screams of those within. My blood seemed to freeze in my bones. Our line slowed as we got to the gate.

Cutch glanced at me, 'All right?' he asked.

There was no answer to that.

We could not even walk down the streets. The wounded had been trampled by hooves or cut down where they stood. Whether they were our men or theirs, there was no telling. They lay crumpled like litter where only a few weeks before they had been shopping for gloves, or buying the family dinner.

A group of six cavaliers were advancing towards us, their swords brandished before them. They were clearing the road of bodies, kicking or hauling them out of the way. A woman wept, rocked back and forth in the dirt, eyes glazed in terror, hanging on to her injured husband.

With a jolt I recognised her – the woman with yellow hair, the one I'd shared a crust with. She was crouching over one of our men. He was groaning, holding onto his belly where his buff coat bled, wet and red. Stomach wounds were the worst. He was a goner. The enemy were grouping together, they'd seen us.

'Don't fire. Wait for reinforcements,' Cutch hissed.

We were outnumbered. I looked over my shoulder, but there was nobody there to help us.

When I turned back I recognised Copthorne as one of the men. He seized the woman by her yellow hair and yanked her to upright. She pressed her hands together to her chest in supplication, but he ignored the gesture and pushed his blade up under her chin.

'Please, Sir,' she gasped.

'Say "Sir" again,' he said.

'Sir, have mercy.'

Copthorne saw me coming. He held the woman there an instant longer, then swiftly thrust the point of his blade through her chest; let her sag and fall.

He was about to go for me, when one of his cavalier companions caught him by the sleeve, 'Leave it!' he yelled. 'Clear the streets, those were our orders!'

A trumpet call, and Copthorne turned abruptly away from us, loped away back down the street beckoning to his men. His friends rolled the bodies of the soldier and his wife to the side of the gutter, as if they were hauling carcasses at an abattoir, then continued their grisly business of clearing the rest of the road.

I ran to the woman. She was alive, but the wound was fatal. 'Please,' she said, begging me with her eyes, 'your gun.'

'I can't,' I said. What she was asking was too much.

But her eyes still begged me, her pain cut me like a hot knife. I took a deep breath.

'Lord have Mercy,' I whispered. I fired at point blank range.

A few moments later I reloaded, finished her husband and another poor old man who lay groaning in his own blood in the gutter.

'What the hell are you doing?' Cutch tried to pull me away.

'Sparing no soul,' I said grimly, ramming more wadding into my gun, 'that's what our orders are.'

He stilled my arm. 'Don't be crazy. Save your powder, these aren't worth it.'

'Not worth it? Not bloody worth it?' My words were thick with rage. 'Leave go of me.' I thrust him away. 'D'you want them to die in slow agony? These are our countrymen.' I fired my gun at a Royalist soldier, whose stomach was no longer in his skin. The shot went through his skull and he lay still.

Tears blurred my eyes.

I was about to fire again when a troop of horsemen appeared at the top of the street. I glanced round. They were Royalists, and something about their demeanour told me they meant business.

'Ralph! Get a grip.' Cutch shook me by the shoulders.

'God Save the King!' came a yell behind us.

I swiveled to see the six men who had been clearing a way, running back towards us. Cutch side-stepped neatly into an alley, dragging me with him.

In a flash of understanding, I realised the rider bearing down on us was the young King Charles himself, though we should not call him that. He was nobody, I had to remind myself. His father had been beheaded and we no longer had a king.

His fine-boned horse passed within a few feet, close enough for me to see his polished-leather boots with their fall of pristine lace dangling over the tops. The whiteness and delicacy of that lace was out of place in this street of carnage. He was a youth my age, but whippet–thin, his pale face blank. He averted his eyes from the dead men piled up to the shop doors.

I wanted to shout at him – look at them! This is all for your cause!

The group of foot soldiers ran to the empty mounts that jostled behind the party. Copthorne spotted us in the alley, and from his eyes I could see he was still intent on attacking me. He unsheathed his sword and sprinted towards us.

'Copthorne. To Horse. Now.' The Royal equerry pointed to the empty steed he was leading, a big black beast with foam-flecked reins.

'I'll find you, Chaplin,' Copthorne hurled the words at me, 'when this is over, I'll find you and make sure you're planted so deep in this earth no-one will know where to look for you.'

I stuck one finger up at him. 'Go tup yourself!' He was a madman; I'd seen enough of him to know he'd lost his wits.

'Copthorne!' The equerry called again.

Ahead, the young King was looking over his shoulder with disapproval.

Copthorne's face twisted into a tight knot. Reluctantly, he vaulted astride the horse and kicked it forward.

I watched him go, wondering why he should have taken it upon himself to make such a personal vendetta of this war.

The rumble from the square warned of the approach of the Parliament cavalry. I turned. They were galloping towards the gate to cut off the Royal party's escape. We let out a cheer of jubilation, but it was short-lived. At the last minute a ramshackle cart pulled by two huge oxen trundled out of the side street.

It had all been planned, that much was obvious. Our cavalry could not pass, and the driver of the cart skittered away, head down, into one of the nearby houses. Meanwhile I watched in frustration as the retreating Royalists and their whippersnapper of a king jostled their way down the side street towards St Martins Gate.

Just before they clattered out, Copthorne swiveled on his horse. His eyes met mine in a savage smile. 'For God and the King!' he yelled. But it was a threat, not a call to arms.

CHAPTER FOUR

An Invitation

The tavern was cramped and the floor swilling with beer despite its layer of straw. Cutch and I sat near the door to take advantage of the draught. The day was hot and airless, and we stank of sweat and the hollow depression that hung in our heads. So many dead at Worcester. Too many to bury. Father still rotting where he fell.

We were given leave and ordered to march home to await more instruction, but we all knew it was over. England was on its knees with fighting, too many men had seen too much. Halfway home, and even now none of it seemed real.

We'd been sent on our way with the words of Preacher Peters in our ears – stirring words which told us Worcester was 'where England's sorrows began, and where they were happily ended.' Happily.

What a jest. Preacher Peters had obviously been nowhere near any battlefield. Nine years to the day, he said it was, in that very spot, that the fighting had begun. A picture arose of my father, ruffling my hair, showing me how to cast a line for a fish, before all this started. I mourned them both, despite myself; the boy and the father who were lost. Though truth be told, I had lost my father to the liquor bottle even before the war.

On the table next to us an old soldier turned to me, waved a pamphlet under my nose, 'All this bloody fighting, and what do they want? They want their old England back, that's what.'

'That can't be true,' Cutch said.

''Tis too. They want it back how it was before. Back to the 'Good Old Days'. It was all a waste of time. Nothing will ever change. No wonder I want to get bloody drunk.' He stood unsteadily, and staggered out of the door, leaving us to ourselves.

Cutch passed me the jug of ale and I poured a fresh tankard. Cutch was pale and exhausted, his cheekbones making stark hollows above sunken cheeks. The fire of battle had gone from his eyes. He rested his skinny arms on the table and hung his head.

'If it's really over,' I said, 'what will you do?' I'd got used to him, to his company.

'Don't know. I've forgotten everything I used to know about the wheelwright's trade. Wouldn't know a spoke-shave from a stick, now. But I'm pretty handy with the old surgeon's blade, so I guess set up somewhere as a barber-surgeon.'

'Have you no family?'

'Never did have. Parents both dead of the plague when I turned twelve.'

'Must have been hard, that.'

He brushed away my comment. 'Nah. But it was a relief to join up. I was sick of being pushed from pillar to post. Started as a messenger boy. Been with the army ever since.'

'Where are you from?'

'Wiltshire. But the army's my family now. Reckoned I should try it, as there was no-one to fret over me. Best thing I ever did. Kept me busy, see. Those who have kin have it hardest in war, I reckon. Anyway, what about you?'

I trailed a fingertip in a pool of beer on the table. 'Can't wait to get home. Back to Markyate and the estate. Everywhere I go I see land falling to thistle and weed. It pains me. With Father dead, I'll take on his portion. Grow crops, a few cows, pigs. Barter a bit. I've got friends who want to work together, in a community, a new way of working. But first there's my mother and my little brother, see. With Father gone, they'll need a man to take care of everything, and I'm going to do a better job than he ever did.'

'Just one brother?'

'No, three sisters as well, God help me. Martha's only five. But the other two have left home. There's Elizabeth — she lives in at the apothecary, and Abigail. She's done well — she's a lady's maid at the big house — Markyate Manor. In fact I have hopes I'll be able to persuade the lady of the manor to let me have land from the estate for our community.'

'That's if she gets to keep her land and isn't deported to be a slave in the Indies.'

I paused, my tankard halfway to my mouth. 'They won't deport women, will they?'

'Want to bet? 'Bout time the aristocracy got a taste of hard work, don't you think?'

'Lady Fanshawe's only seventeen. And she's not...she's not like the usual lady of the manor.' I felt my face flush with heat.

'No.' Cutch stared. 'You don't mean...?'

The familiar ache opened in my chest. I swallowed, looked away.

Seeing my reaction, he shook his head. 'You stupid bugger. Don't let the sergeant find out you've been hob-nobbing with the enemy, he'll wring your stupid neck. Did your Father know?'

'Yes, but it's not how you think. Kate's a—'

'Kate!' He thumped his fist on the table, guffawed. 'Holy God on High, you're even dafter than I thought. Don't waste your time, Ralph. She'll be a pauper like the rest of us soon enough, if Cromwell gets his way.'

'That's just it, she won't care. Money means nothing to her.'

He rolled his eyes. 'Amazing what a pretty face can do. Sounds to me like you've had the wool pulled over you good and proper.' He took another swig of ale. 'She'll never agree to it, a crop of Roundheads roaming all over her land.'

'I thought that at first too. But you're wrong. She's all for change and a better future for all. We met through the Diggers.'

Now Cutch's eyes did widen. 'That bunch of madmen? Winstanley's lot? I thought they'd been well and truly flattened.'

'We nearly were. We tried to build houses on the common land, just outside the village. Equal shares in everything, just like Winstanley preached. There's nothing left now but stones.' I shook my head, 'They beat us off. Folk were scared of us, I reckon.'

I told him how Abigail had brought Kate to the Diggers meetings in disguise, and how we'd fallen for each other.

Once I started to speak, it was as if I'd unlocked a culvert — it all gushed out. I told him everything, right up to how I'd rescued Kate from my drunken father and the Parliamentary Army when they billeted themselves on Markyate Manor.

'You really think she'd turn her estate to the common good?'

'It's complicated. She's heard us all talk at our Digger's meetings—the evils of privately-owned property, of how the land is our God-given right and shouldn't be kept from us by power-hungry lords. And she agrees. But she's married to Thomas Fanshawe. He'll have plans for that land too. His uncle, Sir Simon Fanshawe, wanted him to sell it, use the proceeds to fund the King's Army. But I'm not sure how things will stand now.'

'She's married?' He hit his hand to his head. 'Why does that not surprise me?'

'He's abroad,' I said, 'hiding from the likes of us.' Just the thought of his existence made me want to kick something.

'I'd like to meet this Kate,' he said softly. 'If what you're telling me is true, she sounds like no bleeding aristocrat I've ever known.'

'Come with me then. If you've nowhere else you need to go.'

'Is that an invitation?'

'If you like.'

He grinned, thumped me on the back. 'Well I guess someone needs to keep you safe from the attentions of this lady of the manor.'

CHAPTER FIVE

The Homecoming

When we rode up to Markyate Manor I expected to see the harvest left to rot, but the fields were full of men and women raking and turning hay. I slowed my horse.

'What's wrong?' Cutch reined in beside me.

'Her husband could be back. I don't like the look of it.'

We trotted on slowly until a burly man with a rough, straggly beard and a wide puritan collar stood in the middle of the lane. We had no choice but to stop. 'Can I help you?' His tone was surly.

'I'm here to see Lady Katherine Fanshawe. I'm Ralph Chaplin, one of the tenants. I'm home from the fighting. That's my land over there.' I pointed to where two men were hoeing Father's plot.

'Is that right?' He made no attempt to move.

'What's going on with all these men?' I asked.

'We're having a May ball. What's it look like? Heard tell in the village they needed some help with the harvest,' he said.

'Who's in charge?' I asked. Cutch winced at my manner.

'You're looking at him.' He planted his feet even more firmly in my horse's path. 'Mallinson, the Constable, asked me to come. Said all the menfolk were away fighting and her ladyship's made no provision to look to the herd, or to fix the horses.' He said 'her ladyship' with scorn.

I bristled. 'Well, Lady Katherine won't need your help, now I'm back,' I said, kicking my horse forward, but the man still did not move and I was forced to rein back again.

He smiled. 'Going to do all the harvesting yourselves, are you?' He glanced derisively at Cutch. 'I'll call them off your plot, but there's men and women in the village need work, and I'll not shift them until I get the say-so from Constable Mallinson.'

'What's he got to do with it?'

'We're under his orders. We've agreed to muck out the horses, and the corn in the lower meadow needs cutting today if it's not to spoil. Lady Katherine's like all the rest of the gentry – she's got no real idea about the land, doesn't know chaff from—'

'Ralph!'

The stranger bit off his words, bowed his head. Kate flew down the drive towards me.

I threw myself down from my horse, but did not want to embrace her before that man. Her face had turned pink as a plum, her eyes shone with unshed tears.

'I saw your horses from the window. Thank God,' she said. 'We feared the worst.' She came straight to me, pressed herself into my arms.

I could not resist her, I squeezed her tight to my chest, touched my mouth to her soft copper hair.

In that brief second I caught the other man's eyes, like a bird of prey fixed on a rabbit, but immediately they clouded over into an expression of neutrality. Hurriedly, I released Kate, looked over to where Cutch scraped his boot back and forth on the ground. I shouldn't have kissed her in public.

'This is Cutch, Cuthbert Briggs, he was in my regiment,' I said.

Cutch removed his hat, bowed, tried not to stare at her.

'Welcome,' Kate said, 'any friend of Ralph is a friend of mine.'

'If you'll excuse me, God's work won't wait.' The man who'd greeted us said dourly. He gave a barely perceptible nod and stalked away.

As soon as he was out of earshot I asked, 'Who's he?'

'Jack Downall, one of the men from the village,' Kate said.

So I had a name for the insolent brute at last. 'Whose idea was it for him to bring all these men?'

'Why? What's wrong?' She was defensive. 'Jacob's father sent him. Abigail was keen that we should keep good relations with the Mallinsons. And anyway, It's kind of Mr Downall to offer his help.'

'But why wasn't he fighting? What's he after?'

She looked puzzled, wary. 'After? Nothing. Abi and I can't run this whole estate by ourselves. And until my husband puts another man in charge—'

'But he's not here,' I said. I didn't even want to think about him. 'Anyway, you don't need to employ anyone anymore. I can deal with it, now I'm back.'

'It's a big house,' Kate gestured towards the red-brick towers and lofty windows of the manor. 'Jacob's father's only trying to help. He knows Abi and I couldn't manage the heavy work of the harvest on our own, and when you went to war we'd no idea if…we'd no idea when you were coming back—'

'Shall I take the horses up to the yard and tether them?' Cutch seemed anxious to be on the move.

Kate pointed out the stables, and Cutch led our hired horses away.

'I'm surprised you wanted to put another unknown man in charge so soon,' I said, still grouching. 'Remember Grice.'

'As if I could forget.' Kate twisted her hands together. She looked flustered, her cheeks had coloured up with two spots of red. 'Sooner or later I would have had to employ someone. Why not Downall? He wants the work, and he could be just the luck we need.'

The sun beat down on my head, sweat gathered on my brow. I could not tell her I was disappointed, that I'd hoped it would be me helping her with the Manor, sorting out the manpower, running it the Diggers way, with fair shares for all. I wiped my damp forehead, tried to stay calm, but my voice came out sulkier than I'd intended; 'I don't want any man here telling us what to do,' I said, 'besides, he's brought half the village up here. They'll all be gawping around the estate, poking their noses into our business. We'll have no privacy. And we know nothing about any of them, they could be thieves, or ruffians!'

She gave me a sharp look. 'What's there to steal?' she said, throwing up her hands. 'The Roundheads took everything. And the Constable sent him, don't forget. Jacob's father.'

'We could have managed.'

'How? The only thing we have that's worth anything is the land and the beasts. And they must be worked.' Kate pressed her lips together in a stubborn frown.

I knew she talked sense. Markyate Manor was an empty shell. It had been over-run by the Roundhead rebels on their way south. They had ripped out everything that wasn't tied down, and when I left for Worcester, Abigail and Kate were still scrubbing it clean.

It would take a lot longer to scrub the soldiers' unwelcome presence from Kate's mind. The memory of my father's attempt to ravish her made me catch my breath, but I quashed it.

He was dead. No point thinking of him.

Kate's eyes burned with righteous unshed tears. 'I thought you'd approve. Abigail said you'd want us to do it. "Ralph can't bear waste," that's what she said. And all those families will go hungry if we don't harvest the corn for flour.' She drew herself up tall, 'It's my responsibility, as the lady of the manor, don't you understand?'

Lady of the Manor. How I hated that label. It stood for everything I loathed. It did not feel like it belonged to my Kate, the Kate with the zeal for change and a new world of free and equal men.

All I wanted to do was hold her tight, but somehow I couldn't reach for her, not now there was disagreement between us. The familiar chasm was opening in my heart; Kate folded her arms defiantly across her chest as if to shut me out. My homecoming was going wrong already.

I swallowed, tried to rescue the situation. 'You're right. Abigail wouldn't want us falling out with Jacob's father; that much is certain. She's sweet on Jacob, I know. And I suppose it can do no harm to give Downall a trial.'

No harm. But I didn't know then how convoluted life is, how one thing falls into another, like a single stone cast into a pond.

We walked slowly up the drive. I was embarrassed at my blood-spattered clothing, my bruised face. They were things I could do nothing about, but being next to Kate in her white muslin neckerchief and her blue sprigged summer gown, I felt dirty and unkempt, and more like a farmer's son than ever. The knot of fear that I wasn't quite adequate, that I was below her station, silenced my conversation.

I followed her up the road feeling like a servant. But the sight of her small feet in their dainty kidskin shoes on the rough stones of the drive filled me with a sudden rush of pain. I wanted to hold her feet in my hands, kiss each white toe. But I said nothing, she must already be thinking me boorish and rude.

When we reached the yard she pulled open the door to the kitchen. 'Come within,' she said.

She drew a chair out at the scrubbed wooden table, and I threw off my bags and weapons.

We stood a moment, both awkward, unable to say what we really wanted. 'Are you alright?' I managed. My eyes searched hers.

'The better for seeing you.' She smiled, and it was like a spatter of sunshine. 'But you missed Abi, she's gone to the market to fetch more yeast for brewing and baking.'

'How is she?' I was anxious for news of my sister.

'Same old Abigail. Sharp as a tack and stubborn as a mule. But Lord, how she works. I could not manage without her.' Her green eyes caught me with their arresting light.

I rubbed my index finger along the edge of the table, searching for the words. 'Father's dead. I'll have to break it to her.'

'Oh, Ralph. I'm sorry.'

'Don't be. He treated you foully. But I'm dreading giving Abigail the news, she loved him right enough. And I'll have to tell my mother, too. Heaven alone knows how she'll take it.'

We sat at the table whilst I told Kate what had happened to Father. I skirted the detail, because I couldn't speak of it, the words choked me. I tried to tell her without emotion, but my eyes betrayed me. A tear sneaked out from somewhere. Annoyed, I brushed it away, glad Cutch could not see. He'd had the good sense to leave the pair of us alone.

Kate listened but said nothing, just reached her hand to cover mine gently, her touch gentle as a snowflake falling. When I fell silent, she pulled me towards her to comfort me, but a flame of desire made me groan. I pressed my mouth onto hers. Her lips were soft and yielding. She smelled of sweet hay and sunshine. Her arms crept around my waist and we held each other a long while whilst I stilled the beating of my heart. 'Dearest Kate,' I said.

'Don't be in too much of a hurry to step into your father's shoes,' she said softly. 'It can wait. You have your mother to think of, and grieving takes time.'

'I suppose I must ride over to tell her.' I dragged my mind back to the practicalities.

'Later. Downall's taken care of your old horse, Titan, whilst you were away, he's still stabled in the yard.'

I scowled. I didn't want Downall anywhere near my horse. I was reluctant to let the business of Downall go, but as Kate talked of Abigail and the running of the house, and how hard it was for just the two of them to see to all the chores, I softened.

Her fingers pulled at her curls in worry, so I reached up to take hold of her hand. Her eyes met mine. Again, that peculiar sensation, like falling. I could not drag my eyes away. My mouth turned dry, I swallowed.

Kate's green eyes never left my face. 'It's so good to see you safe,' she whispered.

'You look beautiful,' I said. And she did. My memory of her could never compare with the real thing, the faint dust of freckles over her nose, the lustre of her copper-coloured hair.

I reached out for her again, and she wrapped her arms around my back. I kissed her neck over and over, tasting her skin, salty with damp from the heat. She buried her head into my shoulder, and I gripped her tighter, pulled her forward until she straddled my thighs, her thick skirts and petticoats bunched against my knees.

An urgent need rose in me that made my breath shallow and thin.

'Ralph?' she said, her hands tightening and pushing on my shoulders.

Reluctantly I let go. 'What is it?'

'I...nothing.' A shadow passed over her expression.

'Tell.' I shook her gently to try to get an answer but she inclined her head.

'My husband...' her voice was so faint I could barely hear it.

The kitchen door creaked open, and she leapt away from me, fear flaring in her eyes.

It was Downall. His smirking face showed he had seen us, closer than we should be for decency.

'I can't get the stooks in,' he said. 'Rain's coming and we need more hands. That is, if you've not got more important things to do.'

Insolent dog. He would never have dared to speak to Lady Katherine Fanshawe that way before Cromwell's victory.

'I'll come,' I said tersely, 'and Cutch will help us. He's in the stables.'

'We'll need all hands. Women too.' He looked pointedly at Kate with his pale grey eyes, his thumbs stuck in his breeches, his shirt patched with sweat. It looked like it would please him to see Kate work, but for all the wrong reasons.

'It's all right,' she said, glancing at me reassuringly. 'Certainly, I will lend a hand.'

A crack of thunder. The first big drops of rain began to fall, soaking my shoulders as we scurried to load the corn into the barn. Kate waited to hold the door ajar whilst the rest of us ran back and forth across the slippery yard with armfuls of sheaves.

It was nearly all in when the heavens split open and rods of rain like arrows pelted down on us. Ducking and squealing, the workers dived for shelter.

We found ourselves all huddled together like sheep inside the barn. I could not help but notice that the farmhands were surly with us, as if our presence displeased them. Mostly ragged women, and old wizened men, in dark puritan clothes, they hugged their skinny arms across their chests.

'Just in time,' Cutch said, looking brightly around him.

'Thanks to us,' Downall said. 'Mallinson was right. It would have spoiled for sure without us.'

'It would have been quicker with the cart. If she'd thought to have the wheels mended.' A woman with straggly hair pointed at Kate.

'Show some respect,' I said. 'It's Lady Katherine Fanshawe you're addressing.'

'There won't be any Lady 'this' or Lord 'that' no more,' she said. 'She'll be off this land, soon as there's a Parliament writ from Cromwell. Mallinson told us we'd better look to ourselves. We could wait months before they decide what to do with the place. And then what would happen? The harvest would spoil, and we'd all go hungry, that's what.'

'Mallinson said that?' Even as I said the words, I could well believe it. Jacob's father would want what was right for the village. He would never consider the Fanshawe's rights. Like all of us, he was an entrenched supporter of Parliament.

'No order has yet arrived,' Kate said, eyes flashing, 'and until that time, the Fanshawes own this land and will decide what to do with it.' Her chin was up, her mouth set in a firm line.

'And you'll make us, will you?' Downall said.

'Just a minute.' Cutch inserted himself between Kate and Downall. 'You said the cart's broken. I can fix it if you like. I used to be a wheelwright.'

Part of me knew Cutch was trying to divert us, but I did not listen. 'The sheaves can stay in this barn until we know what is going to happen,' I said, stepping forward.

'And what's it to you?' Downall's voice was almost a snarl. 'Got up the girl's skirts have you?'

'Take that back!'

'Whoa!' Cutch said, glaring at Downall. 'This man was on the battlefield at Worcester for your cause! Do you dare to insult him—?'

'Keep out of it, you,' Downall snapped. 'It's none of your business.'

'Please, Ralph?' a restraining hand on my arm.

I turned in frustration to see my sixteen year old sister Abigail, returned from the market, her wet hair hanging round her face. Her expression showed me she had not understood what was happening, could not lip-read these angry men. I drew her into a hurried embrace to reassure her.

But it was of little use, Cutch had his fists up already, his eyes fixed on Downall.

'What's it been bloody for?' Cutch said. 'For cowards like you? You don't know the half of it, sitting here waiting for us to do all the fighting for you.'

Downall took a swing at Cutch who dodged and his fist nearly connected with my shoulder. Days of battle had made me jumpy, my fist shot out before I had time to think, but I was too far away. Downall leapt forwards, punched me in the eye.

A collective intake of breath.

Half-blinded, I whipped out my sword, but he was too quick and his second blow caught me full on the mouth.

'You dare to draw swords here?' Kate's icy voice.

I was only barely aware of the hands pulling me back. With a supreme effort I withdrew.

'We will have order!' Kate cried. 'Are you men or beasts?' Her words cut the air with their intrinsic authority.

Cutch took hold of my arm, whether to restrain me or prop me up, I didn't know.

'You fool!' Abigail's eyes were accusing, as she took in my bare blade.

Kate turned her gaze to me. Her face was controlled but her eyes were black with fury. 'Work is over for the day. Get to your homes. There's enough fighting on the battlefield without any of you bringing it here. Now go.' With that she stalked out of the barn.

I hastily sheathed my sword and followed her but she was too fast for me. She hitched her skirts and marched across the soaking stubble towards the house. Abigail threw up her hands at me with an expression of disgust, and went hurrying after her.

'We cannot leave them alone in the house,' I said to Cutch thickly, through my swollen lip, 'They are only women.'

Cutch was reluctant to let Downall be. 'Who does he think he is? Too cowardly to fight, but wants to do it in his own back yard!'

His blood was up. I dragged Cutch out by the arm and set off after Kate and Abigail.

When we got inside there was no sign of either Abigail or Kate. We bolted the doors, fearful we were outnumbered and that if Downall had a mind, he and the harvesters would come after us. Cutch kept an eye on the window. 'They're leaving,' he said.

I peered out over his shoulder. The crowd of workers were slouching away down the drive, heads bent against the driving rain. Downall walked slowly, his gaggle of hangers-on fawning on his words. We could not hear what he said, but it was clear it was not good. He kept glancing at the house and scowling.

I shot back out of view, shivered, lifted my hand to my face. My eye was tender and blood had dried in a crust over the bruise on my mouth. Another battle scar to join the others, but this time from closer to home.

The house was quiet, but once or twice I could hear muffled female voices echoing above. Eventually I heard footsteps on the stairs, the door burst open.

'She won't come down,' Abigail said. 'Why must you always do this?'

'A fine welcome it is then, for your brother home from the war.'

I tried to embrace her but she pushed me away. Abigail had read my lips, I knew, but she walked away to the window, turned her back to me.

I stared at her neat back, the tightly-tied bow of her apron for a moment before I followed her, took hold of her by the shoulder, spun her round, 'Abigail...Father's dead,' I said.

She searched my face, saw the pain, the tangle of emotion etched there. 'No,' she said.

I nodded my head, held out my arms, but she kept her distance.

'No. You're wrong. He'll be captured somewhere, like last time.'

I slowly shook my head. 'I saw him die.'

Her eyes raked my face again, and seeing the truth, she turned ashen. She said not a word. Instead, she turned, walked like a sleepwalker to the door, twisted the handle, pushed. The door would not open. She needed to pull, not push.

'Wait!' I cried.

She jerked the door back and it almost hit her in the face. But she hardly noticed. She hurried out and I heard the increasing speed of the tread of her boots all the way up the stairs and along the corridor. Moments later, I winced at the slam of an upstairs door.

I stared round the empty kitchen, then reluctantly put my hat upon my head, picked up my weapons. I would not need them where I was going, but did not want to leave them where that rogue Downall might find them. Puritan or not, he had a temper to match my own.

I picked up my sword and slid it from its scabbard to look at it. I shouldn't have drawn it on Downall, I knew. I fingered the cold hilt; an elegant swirl of etched steel.

A shiver whistled up my spine. Maybe it was bad luck.

It was the sword belonging to Copthorne's brother – the one that Cutch had taken from the battlefield. I sheathed it hurriedly. Tomorrow I'd give it back to Cutch. I could not help wondering if

Copthorne had forgotten me by now. Wherever he was, I wagered he was having a better homecoming than I was.

CHAPTER SIX

Sisterly Love

Cutch and I rode over to Mother's cottage in the dusk. The thunderstorm had left the tracks wet and the gateways were churned with mud.

Mother knew straight away from my face that father was dead. She seemed to be expecting it. Her face was already grey and haggard as if she had not slept.

'Black crows came three nights ago to roost on my roof,' she said. 'I knew then.' She sat us down in the parlour, put her hand to her forehead. 'I don't know how we'll cope. Will they take you on, Ralph? If no man of mine is working for the Fanshawes, they'll not let me stay on at the cottage.'

'Don't worry, Mother, I'll see you can stay.'

'Have they got someone in charge there now since Grice?'

'Yes, Downall from the village. A Puritan. Do you know him?'

'Jack Downall?'

'Big man with sand-coloured hair, heavy jowls?'

'Aye, that's Jack Downall, but he wasn't a Puritan last time I looked.' Mother's face showed she did not like him. She lit up the rushlights to fill the cottage with flickering light. 'He likes to throw his weight about, be the cock of the roost. And he's always got some great cause he's shouting over. Always was a one for speaking atop a tub, was Jack, even as a lad.'

Cutch and I grimaced at each other. 'Well he seems to be a Puritan now,' I said.

'Sounds likely. He'll be on whichever side lines his pocket. And he's never liked us, not these last twenty years. He offered for me before your Father did, see, but my parents turned him down. He's not forgiven either of us. Bitter, he is. When our house burned down he came with the rest of the village but he didn't lift a finger, just stood watching in his smock, pipe stuck out of his mouth. It couldn't mask his smile. He'd see me out of this neighbourhood altogether if he could.'

I sat down, leant my elbows on the table. 'I'll talk to Kate, I mean Lady Fanshawe. She'll make sure you're looked after, Mother; she's soft-hearted - not like her kin.' Even to speak of her brought heat to my face.

Cutch looked away, embarrassed, but even in this light my mother had seen my red face and Cutch's meaningful look.

She frowned. 'I hope you're not getting any ideas, Ralph Chaplin. Thomas Fanshawe and his uncle are not men to cross.'

'They won't be back,' Cutch said, 'Not if they've got sense. They'd be fools to show their faces till the heat's cooled. Cromwell will have them transported, soon as look at them, like all the rest of the King's sympathisers. Mind, I wouldn't wish that on any poor sod. I've seen the boats – stinking great carcasses, full of the court's minions, bound for slave labour. Such a caterwauling and complaining, you never did hear.'

Mother frowned at Cutch as if it was his fault. Then she sighed. 'What will happen to us all? Land needs experienced men to look to it, or where will we be? I hate all this uncertainty. I just want things back how they were.'

Cutch threw me a look, as if to say, 'told you so.'

Just then my little sister Martha came running in. She'd seen our horses.

'Ralfie!' She jumped into my arms and I swung her round. Then she hid behind me, peering out at Cutch.

Cutch gave her a gap-toothed grin and she retreated again, her finger in her mouth in her old childish gesture.

Cutch stuck his thumbs in his ears and waggled his fingers at her until she giggled.

'Would you mind waiting outside a few moments?' Mother said coolly to him. 'Ralph and I need to talk – alone.'

Cutch masked the hurt on his face by bowing too low, and then hurrying out. As soon as he was out of the door Mother said, 'Who on earth is he? Where's he from?'

'Cutch? He's a good friend. Someone Father asked to keep an eye on me.'

'Cutch!' Martha repeated. 'Cutch, Cutch, Cutch!'

'Well I don't want him here,' Mother said, slapping at Martha's skirts.

'Why?'

'Anyone can see he's as common as they come. He probably can't even read. He's not fit company for you, not if we want to maintain any form of social standing in this county. Can't he stay somewhere else?'

I sighed. 'Oh Mother, we have no social standing, have had none these last five years. Not since we lost our house. Cutch is a good fellow. You just don't know him yet. Father said he saved his life.'

She sniffed, tears were threatening to break through. 'Well he failed this time, didn't he?' she whispered. Her bitterness was replaced by entreaty, 'Was it quick? Just tell me it was quick.'

'Instant,' I lied. 'A round of gunfire. He died bravely.'

I took father's signet ring from my pocket and gave it to her, eliciting more weeping. After I had comforted her, and persuaded her that Cutch and I could both stay under her roof, for the time being at least, she asked me about how Downall had come to be at the Manor.

I told her that Constable Mallinson had sent him, to save the harvest. 'See this?' I touched my swollen mouth. 'Downall did it. Punched me.'

She swayed back in horror. 'Not from fighting the King's Men, then?'

'No. Downall went for me. He was rude to Kate...I mean, Lady Fanshawe, and he was spoiling for a fight.'

'Lord have mercy. Same old Jack. Then you'd better apologise and try to get along with him if you can, if Constable Mallinson sent him. Grease the wheels a bit. You know Elisabeth's set her cap at Jacob Mallinson?'

'Elizabeth?' It didn't make sense.

'Don't look like that, Jacob's not a bad catch.'

'But Mother, it's Abigail that Jacob's keen on, not Elizabeth.' But in an instant I'd realised. Curse Elizabeth. She must have got wind of the fact that Abigail and Jacob were close. Trust her to want to ruin it all.

'But Elizabeth said—'

'Oh Lord. Can't I be away two minutes, but Elizabeth makes more trouble? I'll have to speak to her.'

'Is Liz'beth coming?' asked Martha, twirling a drop-spindle round and round, 'will she bring sweetmeats?'

'No, peachkins. Not today.' Mother turned to me again, 'Elizabeth said Jacob would be calling, and when he did, I must be sure to give my permission to court her, at least until Father came home. But now of course, he won't be coming back. So don't you go upsetting the applecart by falling out with Downall and Constable Mallinson. Jacob's of a good family; Elizabeth could do much worse. And he seems nice enough, now the pair of you have given up those foolish Digger notions.' I stood up to object but she waved her hand at me, 'Enough Ralph. I know what I'm talking about.' She rubbed her temples with her fingers. 'I daresay the courtship will have to be longer now before they can be wed. We've no dowry saved, and I'm afraid it will be up to you as man of the house to see what you can do for Elizabeth and Abigail.'

I sat down heavily. It had never occurred to me that now Father was gone, I'd be responsible for my sisters. 'I hope they'll be patient then,' I said. 'It could take years, and I'm not sweating my guts out for one of Elizabeth's cock-eyed notions. She *knows* Abigail likes Jacob. That's why she's doing it.'

Mother sighed. ' Oh Ralph, I don't care which one Jacob chooses, just so long as it's one of them.'

'You know that's not true.'

She shook her head. 'I've enough to worry over with Martha and William.' She gestured at the cradle where William was still sleeping despite our raised voices. 'See what can be done, would you, Ralph dear. And Ralph...' My heart dropped into my boots, she had the warning tone I remembered from being a small boy. 'Talking of suitors....No taking liberties with the Fanshawes. Find yourself a nice, middling girl. None of us know how Cromwell will deal with it all, and meanwhile, the Fanshawes are our bread and butter. She might appear friendly enough, but don't be getting too familiar with Lady Fanshawe. One wrong foot and she could have your head on the block quicker than—'

'Enough, Mother!' I thumped my fist on the table. 'Must I hear nothing but do's and don'ts? Father's not yet cold in the earth and you must nag at me like a weaver wife.'

My harsh words brought out fresh tears. Mother pressed the sodden kerchief to her still-red eyes, and I felt terrible then, to have been so unkind. I walked to the window to hide my discomfort. From there I could see the lonely figure of Cutch, still waiting disconsolately on the woodpile. A great lump of gristle seemed to have lodged in my throat.

I turned back to see Mother weeping into her folded arms. I went over to rub her shoulders. 'I'm sorry; I didn't mean to be so sharp. The soldiers pulled up everything edible and I don't know if I can make enough from the land to support us. Not if the girls need dowries. I haven't even enough coin to buy you a mourning gown.'

She blew her nose. 'My church black will do.'

''Course it will. But I'd like you to have better. And you mustn't worry. It's for me to deal with, I'm the man of the house now. I've told Lady Katherine I'll till Father's land, and take on more acreage too if she'll see fit to give me care of it.'

'And will she?'

I looked at my knees, aware that Kate might hand it all over to Downall. 'I'm sure she will.'

'And you'll be polite to Downall?'

A nod was the best I could manage.

'Then I'll to bed. Douse the lights for me, will you.'

Outside Mother's cottage Cutch was still sitting on the log-pile in the growing dark, shoulders slumped. I wasn't the only one who had received no welcome, I realised.

'Come on, Cutch. Pay no mind to my mother; she's just taken Father's death hard. She'll be glad to have us both to help out, she said.'

'Really?' Cutch looked doubtful.

'Come back inside. You've a place near the fire, and welcome.'

'Hope it's not lit,' he said his white teeth grinning in the gloom, 'I'm sweltering.'

I rested my hand on his shoulder, and pushed him indoors. I could not wait to lie down, but though coming home had exhausted me, I could not sleep. There was so much to think about, and my heart still ached for Kate. Seeing her had only made my longing more intense. I marvelled that a woman could do this to a man, make him feel like his insides had been mysteriously re-arranged.

Cutch and I slept on the flag floor of the cottage that night, neither of us easy. I had thought to come home and find Kate and Abi alone, as they had been when I left, and that I'd advise Kate on what was best for the Manor. Now Downall had squeezed his way into the Manor like a cuckoo in the nest, and I could not help resenting him. And terrible to admit, but I'd had hopes that Kate's husband, Sir Thomas, would have been cut down in a skirmish or, better still, transported to Barbados. Or at the very least, that he'd been imprisoned somewhere a long way away.

Cutch too was restless. He was unused to sleeping indoors, having been on the march for so long. He would not leave his weapons aside, and slept with his head on his bag of powder and match. Poor fellow, I had brought him with me to show him some home comforts, yet my family had failed to give him any sort of welcome. And I still had Elizabeth to deal with.

The next morning I was up early to talk to Mother and help her prepare a hasty breakfast of bread and curd cheese.

When she'd taken Martha out to feed the hens, I said to Cutch, 'Better eat something before we do anything else. I've to go and see my other sister, and I'll certainly need fortification before I do it.'

'Is this the apothecary's assistant?' Cutch asked.

'Elizabeth, yes. She's got a right temper, and I don't know how she'll react when I tell her Father's gone, and I'm the one who's to somehow find her a dowry.'

'Oh Lord.' Cutch understood right away. 'Thank God I've no sisters.'

Once we had eaten and drunk our way through a half-jug of small beer, we mounted up, and rode the eight miles to the apothecary's in Wheathamstead.

Elizabeth was behind the counter, in front of the rows of bottles, grinding up a tincture in a mortar. When she heard us enter she turned, pursed her lips.

'You're back then.'

I nodded. 'This is my friend Cuthbert,' I said, 'Folks call him Cutch.'

Elizabeth ran her eyes over him with an assessing look in her glittering brown eyes, then ignored the introduction. She brushed a few flakes of herb from the counter with her long slim fingers.

'If you've come to tell me about Father, I already know,' she said, tossing her dark curls. 'Everyone in the village knows. One of Father's pikemen made it home.'

'Oh.'

'Will there be a wake?' Elizabeth asked, 'Has Mother said?'

'No.' I told her how I'd assumed he was buried on the battlefield with the rest. 'So she says she doesn't want a fuss, or the expense.'

Elizabeth twirled a finger in one of her side-curls as she took this in. 'Parson says there's to be words said for the fallen. In Church, Sunday. Folk will keep on telling me, like I should be there. Will you go?'

'I expect so.'

She picked up the mortar again and began to bang the pestle down into it. 'Well I'm not going. He was a useless Father; did nothing but drink our wealth away, what little there was left of it.' She glowered in disapproval. 'I'll not sit there and pretend he was a saint. Besides, I've no decent black, and I don't want to be the laughing stock of the village in these work-a-day skirts.'

What was it about women and their clothes? Elizabeth looked immaculate as usual; her lilac cotton gown showed no sign of wear and had been fashionably re-trimmed.

'You look fine to me,' I said. 'What you're wearing won't matter. It's about paying respect.'

'Not just your father, but respect to the whole regiment,' Cutch said.

Elizabeth looked at him with distaste and went back to pounding. 'I haven't time to stand chattering to you. Mr Carlisle's left a long list, and he wants it ready for delivery at noon.'

'I talked to Mother. What's all this about Jacob Mallinson?' I was determined to tackle it.

She stopped pounding and came back to the counter. 'What's she been saying?'

'Come out of the shop a minute, I need to talk to you.'

'About Jacob?'

'Are you coming or not?'

'Not with *him* listening.' She tossed her head in Cutch's direction.

I turned to Cutch. 'You'll mind the shop a moment, won't you?' I asked.

Cutch sighed and went to lean his wiry arms on the counter. I took hold of Elizabeth and dragged her out of the door.

'Let go! You're hurting.'

'Now listen to me, I don't know what game you're playing, but Jacob's set his sights on Abigail, and Abigail's sweet on him—'

'I've no idea what you're talking about.'

'You told Mother he would come courting. How can you do that to your own sister?'

'Jacob likes me,' she said, a sulky look appearing on her face. 'It's not my fault if he finds me more comely than her.'

'I know you, Elizabeth. How you wheedle a man. Abigail won't have many chances, and you're not to foul this up, do you hear?'

'Oh yes, I hear right enough. Abigail's always been everyone's favourite, just because she's deaf. She burnt our house down, or have you forgotten?'

'Don't be foolish. It was an accident. Nobody knows how it happened.'

Elizabeth's face turned mutinous. 'She ruined my life. She destroyed my chances of making a decent marriage.'

'Is that what this is about? That you want to punish her?'

'Father's dead. I knew the stupid sot wouldn't come back. What do you expect me to do? I've got to make my own way now, and if I can make a good match, I will. Abigail can look to herself.'

'You cat!' I said, grabbing her shoulders. 'If I hear you have been trying to take Jacob from Abigail, I'll pull you limb from limb. Do you understand?'

'Don't you threaten me! I'll have Jacob Mallinson if I want, and no-one shall stop me.'

I was at a loss. I knew Elizabeth too well. If you told her not to do something, she'd sure enough be hell-bent on doing it. Getting angry with her would only fuel her determination.

Just at that moment an old gentleman carrying a wicker basket passed by us and pushed open the apothecary's door. We both paused as we heard sharp tinkle of the bell. 'I'll see to it,' she snapped. 'Your thick-headed friend would not have the wit.'

A few moments later Cutch came out of the shop. 'Sheesh,' he said. 'She's something, isn't she, your sister?' His expression was full of admiration. 'No wonder the men are after her.'

I stared at him, unable to believe my ears. 'She's a vixen.'

'But a pretty one.'

I groaned, 'No Cutch, don't even think about it.'

CHAPTER SEVEN

Harvest Home

After our visit to Elizabeth we set of for the Manor to look at Father's strip of land, to see what could be done there. Two acres of ragged corn that needed cutting and then milling for bread, an acre of bald pasture for the pigs, our two horses and the cow, and one acre of weeds that should have been peas and vegetables. Cutch and I walked round it. The rain of the day before had already vanished into the heat haze.

'Dust soup it is then,' Cutch said, scratching his head at the hard-packed earth and scrub before us.

The vegetable patch was empty, marauding soldiers had scavenged anything green. The summer had been dry up until this week, and only the pigs seemed happy, rooting their snouts in the cracks of baked yellow mud.

'We'd best plant anew.' I said, 'I'll see if there's some peas up at the manor. Will you give a hand?'

'Suppose I can turn farmer. Unless another wagon wheel suddenly needs mending. I fixed that one, you know.'

'Oh. Kate will be pleased. We'll walk up there then, see my sister Abigail, and Kate.'

Cutch's face broke into a smile. 'Wondered how long it would be before you found an excuse...'

I cuffed him on the shoulder and grinned.

We had just reached the yard when we heard tramping feet, and turned to see a large body of men heading towards the house. Just the sight of them made my stomach lurch in dread. The last time Cutch and I had seen such a rabble was on the battlefield.

Instinctively I drew myself up straighter. But on closer inspection I saw that it wasn't muskets and pikes they bore, but scythes and hoes. And Downall was at the head of them.

Kate came out of the house, drying her hands on her skirts, to see what was going on. I tried to smile at her, but she ignored me. So she hadn't forgiven me for the fight with Downall. It was humiliating to be passed over by a woman. Kate's attention was focussed on the men gathering on the drive and in the yard before her. There were more men today, and I could see it was a little intimidating.

'Morrow, Milady.' Downall paused, 'I've come to say sorry about yesterday. The heat, it made us all irritable. I was hasty. I've prayed and tried to make my peace with the Almighty. It won't happen again, and I hope there's no hard feelings.'

The rabble behind him stared at Kate silently. Her cheeks blotched red, but she was able to keep her gaze steady. It was a few moments before she spoke.

'You insulted me. It would need more than a few words before I'm prepared to have you work here again.'

I could have cheered. 'I'm sorry, Milady, I—'

'Enough. I don't want any bad feeling between the Fanshawes and the village. I'm anxious to set a good example, to forgive, and move on. I accept your apology, Mr Downall,' she said, 'But who are all these people?'

'Constable Mallinson rounded up these good folks to finish your harvesting.'

Kate scanned the shifting group of surly faces. 'I'm not sure—'

Downall turned his cap in his hands. 'Can't have good food going to waste, Constable Mallinson said.'

Kate looked to me, but I shrugged. I was still sore at her, and even more annoyed that she was still prepared to employ Downall. Her face reddened. 'I'm afraid I cannot pay them,' she said, 'not until Sir Thomas returns.'

'That's easy remedied,' Downall said. 'The sale of the crops should be enough to pay the workers.'

'Who will oversee the selling?' I could not resist chipping in, my wariness showing.

'I've offered, but it's to be negotiated,' he said, eyeing me with cold disdain, 'a matter between Sir Thomas Fanshawe and Constable Mallinson.'

'When was this idea agreed?' I asked.

'By letter. Mallinson wrote to Fanshawe to ask his permission for us to sell the crops, and he sent his signature.'

'I want to see that letter,' I said.

'Ralph...' Kate's face entreated me to leave it.

I sighed, turned away in disgust. In amongst the crowd I spotted John Soper and his son Ned, troublemakers who only a few months ago had tried to put Abigail and Kate in the stocks. The fact that the Sopers were there made me even more uneasy.

'Begging pardon Mistress,' Downall said, 'but if it suits you, we'd best press on. Those clouds over there don't look too friendly, and as anyone will tell you, your corn's almost dried to husk.'

Neither Kate nor I had time to ponder this, as Downall made a signal and the troop followed him through the gate and into the meadow. They stared knowingly at us as they passed, as if they knew about us, about our feelings for each other. Their scornful looks stung like bees, and Kate's face turned pinker and pinker.

Last to go past was John Soper, with his down-turned mouth and stubbled chin. He looked dirty, his shirt patched with sweat and his greasy-kneed breeches held up with twine.

Kate put out a hand to stop him. 'How are you, Mr Soper?'

'Can't complain. And unlike you and your *friend*, your Ladyship, we've got no time to stand about.'

We watched from the gate as Downall gesticulated orders, and the villagers separated to go about their labour.

'Suppose I'd better see to the horses again,' Cutch said gloomily from behind me.

I'd forgotten all about him. 'Right...yes, right.' I was distracted by Kate's nearness. Cutch shook his head at me as he went, obviously disgruntled.

An awkward silence.

Kate turned to me, 'You look like a prize-fighter.' From her tone I knew it was not a compliment.

'Not pretty, hey?' I tried to laugh it off.

She hesitated a moment. 'Ralph, I don't want more trouble.'

I took her hand, squeezed it quickly before letting it go. 'I know. I didn't mean for it to happen.'

'I thought you lived by Winstanley's ideals,' she said, 'of living in harmony together?'

After Worcester, those ideals seemed hopelessly naïve. I rallied myself. 'It's just that we'd come straight from...from...' I shut my mouth. I couldn't tell her. Couldn't even begin to explain what I'd seen. 'Let's not talk about it anymore,' I mumbled.

Kate touched my arm. 'And Ralph, I did think about what you said yesterday. You were right - my husband and his uncle would kill me if they knew I'd let the villagers loose like this on the Fanshawe estate.'

'Then why did you?' I asked softly.

'Abigail. She said I should accept Downall's help if he came back; that we need allies not enemies in the village. That now Cromwell's victorious, it would do nothing for our cause if we set ourselves apart. Besides, she's desperate not to upset Constable Mallinson because of how she feels about Jacob.'

'Where is she?'

'Inside, making potage. She was grieving this morning, so I let her be.'

'I'll go and speak to her.'

'Ralph?' She reached up to gently touch my swollen eye. 'I'm sorry. It's just...I can't bear the thought of more brawling. My uncle used to beat people into his way of thinking with a horse whip. I determined then never to countenance it. ' She turned away, stared out across the land. 'Violence never changes anyone's mind, just drives their convictions deeper. And it's such a waste, when all that power could be used to build something, not knock it down.'

'Don't worry, I'll try to keep civil with him. And I'll speak to Jacob. Find out about this agreement between Constable Mallinson and your husband. Never fear, I'll make sure Downall won't get control of the sale of the harvest.'

She swiveled back, suddenly angry. 'I don't care about the harvest. It can rot for all I care! It's people I care about, don't you understand?'

When she hurried away from me, I had the uneasy feeling I'd failed her again.

Women. They were hard to make out.

Abigail was making potage for the workers mid-day meal. Laid out on the table were some belly pork, chopped herbs, leeks and a batch of dried peas. It still surprised me to see her there in the kitchen of the big house, her sleeves rolled up to the elbows.

'Come to help?' she asked. 'Thought you'd got lost. Is Mother alright?' She did not look at my reply, as if she did not want to hear it.

'Sit a moment,' I said, placing a hand on her arm.

She looked up at me. 'Did you actually see it happen? Father, I mean.'

'Yes.'

'Did we win? Is the young King...?'

'No. He's alive.' I signed, 'Fled into hiding. But Cromwell's victorious. Father's life, well perhaps it was not lost in vain. He died fighting for his cause.'

She stood up again, went to the table.

Chop, chop, chop.

Her hand flashed up and down with the knife, shredding the leeks into tiny slivers. My heart contracted for her. She would not let herself cry.

I went to the cellar and squeezed a few drops of wine from the almost empty cask, put the cup on the table before her.

'I don't need it,' she said, screwing up her nose. 'It's you should be drinking it, not me. You've been to war, seen it happen. I've done nothing, just wait.' She smiled a wan smile. 'Though that was hard enough. But I can't believe he's gone. Can't make sense of it, what it means. And I've got to get this potage finished.' Her words sounded sharp like the chopping.

I sat a while, watching her, until a sob made her shoulders heave. Hurriedly she untied her apron. 'Done,' she announced in a shaky voice. 'I'll just get some air.' She blundered outside, eyes full of tears.

I watched her from the window, hurrying, stumbling across the field, her skirts snagging on the stubble, not knowing where to run to ease the pain, and I sighed, my heart aching for her.

Afterwards I went to fetch Cutch from the stables and we made a start on planting my father's plot. We made good headway, and whilst we dug and tore up weeds I saw it would not take much hard labour to turn around the whole estate, make it productive.

'If we rotated the peas with the turnip crop, and took the bottom meadow for the herd, instead of for hay, that would double our yield in one year. The place needs properly managing, with men who have a real stake in the harvest.'

Cutch wiped his damp forehead with his sleeve, lifted his hat and wafted air over his face. 'Isn't that what Downall's doing? Come on Ralph, leave well alone.'

'He wants control over the price of the corn. It makes me uneasy.'

'Let him get on with it, I say. Haven't we enough to do with all this?' he groaned, waving his hand at the hard ground in front of us.

'The estate's had too many men with no proper plan. Grice was worse than useless, and Downall's just after turning a quick profit. It needs a younger man, with new ideas. Now's our chance, Cutch, to change the old order. I could turn it around, work it on the Diggers' principles.'

He sighed, leant on his hoe. 'You want my advice? Keep to your own business, Ralph, and leave Downall to his. No good will come of interfering.'

'I'm sure Kate would let me try. Divide the land so all who work on it get a share.'

But Cutch had walked away and was scraping at a patch of bramble with his hoe. I eyed his back with frustration. Why wouldn't he listen?

I carried on without talking until the mid-day sun got too warm for us and we went to seek some respite in the shade of the yard. Abigail still had not returned, and I presumed she had gone to see Mother, but Kate was bent over the pan of potage. She poured us some small beer from the jug and we emptied it down our dusty throats in one long draught. A few moments later, Downall stuck his head round the door. He did not knock.

'Have you a large trestle?' he said, 'it would be better for us to eat outside in the air.'

Kate replied there was one in the buttery and I heard the scrape as they brought it out.

When I followed her into the yard as she carried the big pot wrapped in a sack-cloth to keep her hands from burning, it was to see the workers all sitting ready, with their own bowls, spoons and knives laid out before them. One glance was enough to see they were using pews dragged from the Manor Chapel without Kate's permission. Outraged, I opened my mouth to protest, but I clamped it shut. I did not want more trouble, for Kate's sake. Instead I aimed at a mild, 'I'll help to take the benches back to the Chapel afterwards.'

Downall and his men ignored us both, and simply watched as the pot was put on the table. 'Is there no bread?' John Soper asked.

'No. Not unless you bake it yourself,' I growled, unable to conceal my irritation.

'A meal's not a meal with no bread,' he sulked.

Downall gave Soper a warning look. 'There'll be bread once we've got the corn in, isn't that right, Mistress?'

'I don't know,' Kate said, 'We'll have to see what happens when my husband returns.'

'If he returns.' Downall raised his eyebrows, guffawed. The rest of the workers all joined in his laughter but it was not a pleasant sound.

Kate stalked away with her head held high, but her face burning.

I hurried after her, knowing the previous overseer, Grice, had sapped her confidence. The Kate I used to know would have given them their marching orders. This Kate was cowed by them.

It made me ache, beneath the ribs. I'd seen there had been no place left for her at the table, and nobody had moved aside to give her room.

'Don't go back outside,' Kate said, once we were back in the kitchen. 'Stay here, Ralph. We can eat in here, away from their eyes.'

'They insult you. I can't let them do that.'

'No, please, don't make more trouble. My position here is uncertain, and they know it. Their work will be done soon enough. Let's keep the peace a few more days, for Abigail's sake.'

I looked about the kitchen, but there was no food left. Lady Katherine Fanshawe would be eating oatcakes again, despite the fact it was she who had laboured hard over the pot.

The murmur of low conspiratorial voices snaked through the open door, but when Cutch went out to fetch the leftovers, the noise ceased abruptly, and the silence was thick as a grave slab. There was a bristle in the air that made me uneasy. Back in the kitchen I lifted the lid of the pot to see it was scraped clean.

The next day Downall and his men were back as if they were lords and masters, not mere farmhands.

When I went up to the house at mid-day to refill our flagons, I caught Abigail scouring the whey pans in the buttery. She looked even paler than usual in her old black mourning dress that was too small for her. I wore no black. It was a matter of principle, I told myself. Though a tinge of guilt remained.

I helped Abigail lift the heavy pans back onto the stone table. 'I'm worried about Downall,' I said.

Abigail raised her eyebrows, 'Why? He's getting the harvest in. I passed the stables, and he's fed Pepper and Titan and the yard's been swept.'

'No, Cutch did that. He's good with horses. Something doesn't feel right with Downall.'

'You're just nervous because of...because of what happened before when the Roundhead army came. And Father's death, well I suppose it brings it all back.'

'No, it's more than that. He laughed at Kate, they pay her no respect—'

'The old order's crumbling.' She looked up at me, her face grave, her eyes dark. 'Isn't that what you wanted? You can't set her above us one minute and then expect her to be the same as us the next. I hate to admit it, but Grice was right last year when he said Kate will lose her lands. And perhaps Downall knows it.'

'It might not come to that.'

'Well what would you suggest? Mr Know-all? We leave good grain to rot?'

'Downall and his rabble are sitting on the land like vultures,' I said bitterly.

'But it's good news, for you surely? Kate's husband and uncle will stay in exile. Just be patient a while longer, Ralph.'

I knew she was right, but having Downall on the estate was a thorn in my side. 'I've arranged to meet up with the Digger community,' I said casually.

She dropped her scrubbing brush with a clatter. 'Oh Ralph, not again! I'm not sure—'

'I thought it would be good to put our heads together, figure out ways to go ahead, now things have changed. It's time for our ideas to take root.'

'It's too soon. Things will need to settle, and well, we're still in mourning.'

'The meeting's Thursday. In the old barn where we used to meet. I've thought it all out - where the circle of dwellings could go, in the place nearest the river. We could have a real community here – be an example to other landowners of how things could be. As Winstanley said, the land is our common treasury, and we could start right here at Markyate Manor.'

'And what does Kate say to these plans?'

'She's the most convinced of us all, you know that. You'll come, won't you?'

Abigail pursed her lips and picked up her brush, scrubbed at the pan as if it was personally insulting her.

A few moments later she turned, 'If you spent half as much time doing things as dreaming about them, then we wouldn't need to employ men like Downall.'

I said nothing, but her remark stung. I shot out of there and grabbed hold of my spade. I'd show her. For the next half hour I attacked the ground until I'd dug a quarter of an acre over, and my shirt clung clammily to my back.

'What's with you?' Cutch asked when I finally stopped.

'Nothing. And that wheel you fixed on the wagon? It's useless. It's broken again.'

Cutch's face dropped. 'I guess I'm not as good at fixing things as I used to be,' he said. 'Guess I'm out of practice.'

I stomped off up the drive. I'd go and talk to Kate, tell her about the meeting I'd set up, so we could forward our plans for building a Digger community. The war had only increased my determination not to go back to the old ways, and I knew Kate would feel the same. It was just a shame Abigail did not share our vision for the future.

I found Kate in the front drawing room, arranging a bunch of wild meadowsweet and dog-roses in a vase. She turned when she saw me and her face lit up with a welcoming smile.

By heaven, she was beautiful. I crossed the room in a few strides, my errand forgotten, and let her fold into my arms. I inhaled the musky scent of warm skin, turned her face to mine, stroked her cheek.

'It is so good to have you home,' she said, green eyes scanning my face, 'I can't quite believe it. The waiting was so hard. I have to keep looking out of the window to make sure you are really there.'

Home. It felt nice to hear her say the word. Though it would feel more like home, once Downall had gone, and had stopped lording himself about the yard. 'Now I'm back, we can re-instate our Diggers meetings,' I said.

She pulled away, rearranged one of the blooms. 'Mother used to always have roses here, near the window. Shame we only have this old table now, and this jug. But putting them here reminds me of her...of how grand it used to be.'

'Kate, I was thinking, it's not too late to try again with the Diggers community. We could use the land - transform this place, Kate. Own everything in common, like we said we would. Your husband's in exile, perhaps for many years. He won't see what we do.'

She tugged a rose into position in the vase. 'It's complicated. Nothing we do here can be secret; there are eyes and ears everywhere. Word is sure to get back to him, and there are just too many questions. Like, what will happen to the tenants of Markyate Manor?'

I hadn't thought of that. It was a moment before I replied, 'They can join with us in our community.'

'Some may not wish to. Your mother for instance. I can't see her joining the Diggers, can you?'

Kate went to lean on the windowsill, looking out into the garden. She was right about my mother, but I wouldn't admit it.

'I'll persuade her,' I said. 'She'll see it's the way forward, she just needs it explaining.' I put my arms around Kate's waist, rested my chin on her head, twined my hand in hers.

She stiffened. 'You know it's not that easy.'

I turned her to look at me, but her eyes evaded mine. It was as if a sliver of ice had suddenly lodged itself in my heart. 'What are you saying, Kate? How can we go on, unless we build a life together?'

'I don't know.'

Her voice was small, and lines of anguish furrowed her forehead. 'I keep seeing my mother's face, how determined she was to keep the Manor. It was her inheritance, in her family for generations, and I saw the pain she went through to keep he estate intact for me. I can't just throw it away.'

'But a few months ago you were prepared to give it all up and lead a Digger's life.'

'That was then. But we have to face it; the Diggers have failed,' she said. 'Their communities have been razed everywhere they go. Their ideals can't be sustained. Whilst you were away I talked it over with Jacob.'

'With Jacob?' I was stunned.

She pressed on, 'About what sort of England we want, now the royals are routed and we have a chance to change things. We agreed, it's pure folly to think a whole society can live without money, with only barter. And Jacob says Winstanley's views on women's equality – well, Lord knows we need it - but it's too much, too soon. Even Winstanley has had to let it go.'

I could hardly bear to look at her. I was winded, as if someone had punched me. 'But I thought you were…you said you believed in it as I did. Are you telling me it was all a lie?'

'Of course not. I thought I believed it, of course I did, it's just—'

'You said you'd stand by the Diggers creed. That you'd stand beside me on this, as long as we could be together.'

'And I would! But where could we go? Your father was my tenant. You've nothing to inherit, no land—'

'But *you* have. Look at it! There's no reason why the Diggers ideals should not work here.'

'No. It's too dangerous. My husband and stepfather would kill you if they knew you were even talking to me this way. Think! Think of your family, Ralph.' She grasped both my hands, looked up at me with earnest entreaty. 'If I'm careful, don't do anything rash, I can stay here; you can still farm your father's land, and that way I can protect your family. Yours and many others. Your mother relies on me for her cottage, you rely on my for your employment, Abigail is my maidservant, she gets her livelihood from me. It is what common people never understand – that land-owning people like us have responsibilities.'

It was as if she'd slapped me. *Common people?* Heat flared to my face, but I ignored it. I could barely get the words out. 'I'm not good enough for you. That's what you're saying, isn't it?'

Her eyes widened. 'No, of course not, I'm...Ralph! Wait!'

But it was too late I was out of the door so fast I hardly heard her. I snatched up my sword and burst out into the yard. I was in time to see Downall loading up a cart with stooks of hay, but I ignored him. I was too angry to be able to speak.

That night I could not sleep. I tossed and turned until Cutch growled at me to keep quiet and let him get some rest. I'd been so sure Kate would agree. What would I tell Whistler and Barton and the others I'd called to the meeting? I'd look a fool.

It was all Jacob's fault, he'd talked her out of the idea. I'd have to go and see him; see where all this had come from. He'd betrayed me. He was my best friend, and he'd betrayed me.

Cutch rolled over, and his mouth opened in a snore. I prodded him with my boot, and obligingly he stopped. Suddenly I saw him through Mother's eyes, a rough, unkempt mercenary. Everything she did not want me to be. And the worst of it was, I felt more useless than he was. If I couldn't offer Kate a dream, then what could I offer her? Not land or money or skill or status. A view opened up in my mind's eye. I was sowing my father's strip of land, supervised by a smirking Downall. And from the stone terrace of the house, Sir Thomas and Lady Katherine Fanshawe watched me, arm in arm, as I toiled.

No! I leapt up, unable to stand the imaginings of my own mind. I hurried out into the dark, looked up at the pinpricks of stars, paced up and down the lane.

I looked over to where the Manor House must be, but could see nothing, the world was a black hole.

I would not give up. I would marshal my arguments until they were so convincing, Kate would not able to resist them. And I'd talk to Jacob. People were frightened of change; that was all. But I had been at Worcester, and knew that whatever the old way was, if it had led to that, then it was not worth saving. I started to plan my rhetoric, rehearsing my arguments over and over.

CHAPTER EIGHT

Diggers' Dreams

Within a few days Cutch had made himself into the official ostler, dealing with horses, wagons and the sorting out of harness, so as to keep out of Downall's way.

Cutch and Abigail seemed to get along well, and I often saw him help her lift the heavy milk churns or carry her wash tub outside, with much gesturing of their hands, and smiling faces. So I left Cutch trying to mend Abigail's broken yoke whilst I took my horse, Titan, to ride over to confront Jacob.

When I got to Jacob's small cottage I saw a fork stuck up in the earth where he'd been labouring over his vegetable patch, but he was inside, poring over some papers on the scrubbed oak table.

'Ralph!' He was obviously pleased to see me, and scraped the papers into a pile, pulled out a chair.

'Busy?' I asked, but my tone was terse. I did not sit.

He lowered his eyebrows, 'Just a few papers for my father. There's so much more post coming now — instructions about what is and isn't allowed, new laws, new regulations. You know how it is. And Father's not as sharp as he was, needs things explaining sometimes.'

I sat down and leant my elbows on the table. 'Yes, I've come to talk to you about that.'

'Why? What's the matter?'

'Remember when we tried to build our Diggers community on the common?'

He laughed, 'Do I! And we had to run for our lives from Soper and all those men set on giving us a pasting!'

'We weren't for giving up, though, were we?'

Jacob saw my meaning immediately and busied himself again, rubbing his chin with his hand, and shuffling some of his papers randomly about.

I persisted, leaned forward to catch his eye. 'No matter what it took, we said we'd build a new way of living. 'Dig it from the earth itself.' That's what you said.'

'I know. But things are different now,' Jacob said. 'The royals have gone. We have to give Cromwell a chance, see what he'll do for us. He's an ordinary man, a farming man, not an aristocrat.'

'For God's sake Jacob!' I thumped my fist on the table. 'You turned Kate against the Diggers. I can't believe you'd do that to me.'

Jacob stood up, looked me hard in the eye. 'She made her own mind up. Do you seriously think I could persuade Kate to anything if she didn't believe it?' He sighed, shook his head at me. 'We discussed it, yes, but it was nothing personal against you. There's few will stand up for their ideas now. Even old Winstanley himself has given up. And anyway, look at it all.' He patted the papers before him. 'There's so much to do. With all this new legislation, my father needs me.'

'You can't mean it? You're not really going to follow your father's trade?'

'What's wrong with that?'

'It's a merchant's life! Based on gold and greed.'

'My father leads a good, honest life.' His eyes flashed at me, and I realised I had insulted him.

I tried a calmer tone. 'Come on, Jacob, are you telling me you'd really give up the Diggers for a soft living of wool and worsted?'

'I don't know. But Father's getting so the Constable's position is too much for him, and when they elect again, I thought I might stand.'

'You?' I was flabbergasted.

'Is it so surprising?'

'But it's a job for an old man.'

Jacob squared his shoulders. 'Father was my age when he took it on.'

I sat down, put my head in my hands, pressed my fingertips to my forehead whilst I took it all in. A merchant, that was bad enough. But Constable? I thought back to our youth, to Jacob, the rebel I used to know. But then, I realised he was a phantom. It was always me. I was the rebel; Jacob had always been the one offering sensible advice, the one for moderation and hanging back.

'So you see,' Jacob said with a hint of apology, 'if I'm going stand for Constable, it wouldn't sit well to be breaking the law.'

I stared down at the table. 'Kate said you'd had a change of heart, but I didn't believe her.'

'Not exactly a change of heart, just that I'm nearly twenty now – no longer a youth – and there's new priorities—'

'Alright, alright.' I cut him off, stood up again. Was there nobody left who felt the way I did? 'I suppose there's no point in asking if you'll be at the meeting. Day after tomorrow at our usual meeting place - the old barn. Whistler and Barton are coming, and they're bringing some others. Should be quite a crowd.' I was still hopeful.

'Will your sister Abigail be there?'

'Wouldn't miss it,' I said.

'She never mentioned it,' Jacob said. 'Then maybe I might stop by. But I won't be staying. Abigail's one of the reasons I want to stand for Constable. To get a bit more regular money coming in. I have hopes in her direction.'

'I wagered as much. Does your father know?'

'I haven't told him yet, no. But I'm sure he suspects it's a girl that's driving me. She's lovely, your sister. And I can tell she likes me. I was going to ask your father's permission to walk out with her, but since...well, I thought I'd give your mother a bit of time for grieving. I dare say she might take a month or two to arrange her finances and decide on a dowry.'

'Mother's left all that to me,' I said, 'Now I'm the man of the house.'

Jacob frowned. 'What do you mean?'

'Father left her very little. It will be up to me to help our girls.'

Jacob sat down again. 'You're not serious? You can't be expecting Abigail to be wed on what you earn?'

'Why not? Are you saying I can't provide for my own sister?'

'No, no. Course I'm not saying that. It's just a surprise, that's all. And the Diggers lifestyle is not...is not...'

'What?' I stuck out my chin towards him.

'Look, you know what my father's like. He's not an easy man to persuade. He has his own ideas on the sort of girl that...' Seeing my face, his words petered out.

I did not budge.

Jacob sighed. 'From the hints she's let drop, I'd say Abigail's got her heart set on next spring. For the wedding, I mean.'

Oh Lord. That soon. 'I'm glad, Jacob. She'll make you a fine wife. And she'll have a fine dowry too, never you fear.'

He looked at me hard. I'm sure he read the doubt in my eyes, but I blustered my way out of there, taking my leave of him before he had time to consider it more.

All this talk of weddings punched a hole in my ribs, when I could see no future with Kate. Jacob said Kate had made up her own mind about the Diggers, but I wouldn't believe it. It was too frightening to think she would go back to being the Lady of the Manor, and I would be just another of her tenants.

Once I'd left Jacob's I thought about it all the way back to the Manor. I supposed I should be glad about Jacob's plans. I liked Jacob, or at least I used to. And Abigail would be all lit up, I knew. It was just that I didn't know where I was to get the dowry, and I wasn't at all sure I wanted a flaming Constable for a brother-in-law.

On Thursday we met in the barn after the men had finished work and gone home. I'd set out planks on barrels and crates to make a horseshoe of benches. Whilst I impatiently waited for my Digger friends to arrive, Cutch tinkered with the bearing on an axle he was mending. I began to suspect that most of his repairs were in fact bodges. His face was screwed up in concentration as he whittled away trying to fit a wooden peg where it obviously was not meant to go.

Voices from outside warned me of men approaching, and I stood up to greet Barton and Whistler, and two of their friends, raw apprentices by the look of them, and soon there were a scant dozen of us. I noticed Abigail and Kate creeping in at the back, along with Margery and Susan, the other women who supported our cause, and my heart lifted to see them.

Kate was still dressed in a fine gown of some sort of silky shimmery stuff, with her bright hair braided with black lace instead of wearing a cotton coif like the others. It disconcerted me to see her like that. I couldn't get used to it, the fact she was the lady of the manor. Part of me wished she'd worn her homespun like she used to, and been back to the Kate I knew.

'Friends,' I said, when I had gathered their attention, 'Let us pray.'

It had been the Digger's founder, Winstanley, who had set the habit of always starting meetings with a prayer, and I thought it would suit the grand and grave tone I'd planned for my speech.

Dutifully everyone got to their knees on the straw and closed their eyes, even Kate in her fine dress. I had only just begun when I heard a disturbance. I opened one eye to see Jacob sidle in, and sit just behind Abigail. Again I began, but this time I was interrupted by Elizabeth, dressed in a billow of pink muslin, sauntering in like the Queen of Sheba.

God's breath, how had she heard about it?

I snapped both eyes open and glared at her but she took no notice, just swished her skirts to one side and sat down on the rough plank next to Jacob, settling herself, to my mind, far too close.

My voice stuttered as I lost the thread of what I was saying, and I had to make do with a simple hasty prayer instead of the stirring one I'd imagined. Curses. Jacob was smiling at Elizabeth, and poor Abigail would have no idea. Probably didn't hear either of them come in, for she was still fervently praying, a small frown of concentration between her brows.

'Amen,' I finished, aiming a dart of disapproval at Elizabeth.

'Amen,' they toned, Elizabeth's a little too loud so that everyone turned to look at her.

I gathered my scattered thoughts and brought out the plans I had worked on that showed Markyate Manor estate divided up into neat plots, one for each man, and the communal orchards and threshing areas. I outlined the plans, glancing over to look at Kate to see if she understood them.

Her face was immobile as she listened intently to what I was saying. Suddenly I was nervous. I wanted to impress her, prove that I could run the estate better than Downall, build a new world, one better and fairer than before.

In my enthusiasm I spoke too fast, my words tumbling over each other, 'Don't you see? If we can just organise the land, each man will tend his own part, vegetables and peas and a place for chickens to lay, even a pig, well yes, certainly a pig or two...but all will have a share in the produce of the whole. So if one man's harvest fails, he will not starve.'

'But won't it be a deal of work to divide one man's plot from another? Why waste all that labour on building fences?' Elizabeth piped up.

It was unusual for a woman to interrupt in this way. Barton's eyebrows raised, and Abigail turned to see who had spoken. Her face fell, to see her sister sitting so close to Jacob.

'There'll be no fences,' I said. 'The land is not ours to divide. The moles and creatures of the earth don't have such ideas! No, we will take down the fences that divide this land from the rest.'

Kate's forehead furrowed at this, but I carried on. 'Of course I don't deny that every man needs a sense of ownership and pride,' I said, to regain their attention, 'It is good to take care of something and feel it bloom under your hands.'

'I don't see what's wrong with working the land the way we do now,' Elizabeth said. 'Constable Mallinson told me he'd put Mr Downall in charge so that the men could all work together for the good of the village.'

I glared at her. Here I was doing my best to convince Kate, and my own sister was belittling me. But Elizabeth ignored my black looks. She twirled a ringlet between her fingers and said, 'Constable Mallinson was most interested when I told him of your meeting today and these plans Ralph has to share out the Fanshawe land. Constable Mallinson's on some sort of Parliament committee, and said he'd like to be here to discuss it...in fact I'm surprised he's not here already—'

Jacob held up his hand to her, 'Wait!' he said, 'You told my father I was coming here?' He strode towards her, 'When?'

She blinked, 'This morning,' she said as if surprised he should ask. 'He came into the apothecary's a few hours after you did, for a headache powder. I just happened to mention it. You didn't tell me not to. Why? Have I said something wrong?'

She knew damned well she had, but she fluttered her eyelashes artfully and Jacob groaned, 'No, no. It's just, well, I'd told him I was finished with the Diggers.'

'Oh!' Elizabeth's eyes grew round. 'Is that what this is, a Diggers meeting? You never told me that,' she said to me accusingly, using the word 'Diggers' as if it was the work of the Devil himself. 'Is that right, Ralph? The Diggers are illegal, aren't they?'

'Yes,' I was forced to admit. 'But Parliament should never have banned them. What's wrong with a few men meeting together to decide how best to farm their land?'

Cutch was staring at Elizabeth's flushed face with awe, but the other men were shuffling in their seats, faces filled with unease. Whistler had already jammed his felt hat on his head. He tried to catch Barton's eye.

'I reckon if Constable Mallinson's coming, we'd best save our breath for another day,' Barton said.

'He might not come,' I said stubbornly, feeling the meeting, and my chance to convince Kate, slipping from my grasp. 'This isn't strictly speaking a Diggers meeting, just a few friends—'

But the assembled group were already on their feet and making for the back door. And not a moment too soon. I saw Abigail turn to look as she felt the vibration of approaching hoofbeats.

The barn emptied like river water out of a holed bucket. I'd never seen people disappear so quickly.

I peered out through the big double doors at the front. Two horsemen in the meadow. Mallinson must have loaned Downall a horse, for there he was, cantering alongside him, astride one of Mallinson's heavy hunters.

I ran back inside. 'It's them. What should we do?' I asked Kate.

'Nothing,' she said, shrugging her shoulders. 'There's nothing to see. Everyone's gone. Jacob can go out the back way to walk Elizabeth home, and—'

'She can see herself home,' Abigail insisted. 'She got here by herself didn't she?'

'I'll see her home,' Cutch said, holding out his arm, 'It would be my pleasure.' Elizabeth turned her back and ignored him.

'I'll stay and greet my father now he's ridden over,' Jacob said. 'It will give him a chance to meet Abigail again.'

'I'll wait here too, then,' Elizabeth said, 'and you can walk home with me afterwards. It's getting late, and there could be highwaymen abroad. I'll need some protection.'

'Miss Chaplin,' Cutch said, 'I'd be happy to escort you.' His voice was almost pleading.

Outside, I heard the thud of boots as two people dismounted. 'No, Cutch. She's my sister. *I'll* walk her home,' I growled, 'and we're leaving now.' The last thing I needed was another conversation with Downall.

Elizabeth looked sulkily at me, and squirmed away from my insistent grip on her arm.

'Miss Chaplin, I advise you to take up this man's kind offer,' Jacob said, looking at Cutch. 'Although I would be happy to escort you, dusk is falling, I may talk with Father a while, and you have a fair way to travel.'

Elizabeth smiled winsomely at him, though I could tell it cost her dear. 'Very well, I shall take your advice, Mr Mallinson. I look forward to meeting you again. Perhaps I may call you Jacob?' She dipped her head.

'Ho there, Chaplin!' A shout from the threshold. Too late. I couldn't get away now, Jacob's father had seen me. Cutch held out his arm for Elizabeth to take, but she flounced ahead of him out of the back door.

Moments later, the portly figure of Constable Mallinson appeared before us with Downall glowering behind. Constable Mallinson glanced round at the plank benches, but then spotted his son.

'Jacob! I wasn't expecting to see you here. Did we miss the meeting?' Constable Mallinson asked.

'The prayer meeting?' Jacob said, his downcast eyes giving away his discomfort.

'No. The one about the plans for the estate? Elizabeth Chaplin told me there were moves afoot to divide the land.'

'Did she?' Jacob said. 'I don't know where she got that idea from. She must have misunderstood. Sorry if she's brought you here on a wild goose chase. There was a prayer meeting, but it's over. When Elizabeth said you were coming I waited to greet you.'

Downall frowned and glared at me, 'Nobody told me anything about a prayer meeting. You should have told the workers.'

'It was for family and friends only, on account of our losses in the recent wars,' Kate said, putting on her most charming smile. I breathed a sigh of relief. So she was still prepared to defend me against Downall.

'I can't see a Bible anywhere, or any sign of worship,' Downall walked around the barn searching with an eagle eye for anything incriminating. He picked up a hemp jerkin that someone must have left behind in their hurry, and dropped it back on the bench with distaste. 'And a barn is an odd place for worship. It smacks of dissent. Why not use the Manor Chapel, or the church like most good folks?'

'Now Downall, I'm sure there were no dissenters here, not with my son in the party,' Constable Mallinson said.

'Would you care to come into the Manor, sir,' Kate said, hurriedly, 'as you have taken the time to ride over. Abigail will fetch us some cakes and ale.'

Kate did not invite me, but I felt there was nothing I could do but follow everyone inside to the drawing room. I did not trust what might go on behind closed doors.

Mallinson sniffed at the lack of comforts, but Abigail pulled out the best chair for him, and he dusted it down before sitting. Despite Abigail's pretty curtseys and pleasant smile, he ignored her as she brought in the jugs and the tray of tankards, and set them on the table. It was clear he viewed her merely as a servant. I caught her gaze, and she gave me a resigned smile, before sitting quietly near the window, her eyes fixed on Jacob.

Constable Mallinson turned to Kate. 'Lady Fanshawe, I have had an application from your husband to the Sequestration Committee, the committee which deals with the land of the late King's sympathisers. It appears your husband has had a change of heart.' He smiled, waiting for Kate's reaction, but she was silent. 'He now wishes to side with Parliament, in order to retain his lands. He says he's prepared to sign a writ to say he has been misguided and to swear that he will not take up arms against Parliament again.'

'Is that all he must do?' I asked, 'Just sign a paper? He won't be deported?' My heart sank.

'No, it is not as simple as that. There are eight men on the committee and everything about the estate will be weighed in the balance before we agree. And there is the matter of the fee - a third of the yearly tithe. There are also a number of other considerations, such as ensuring the land is managed by someone reliable - someone who will keep Cromwell's Puritan values in mind.'

Downall nodded, and looked smug.

'What will happen to my husband if you refuse his application?' Kate asked.

'He will stay in exile. He will not be permitted to land on English shores again. His estates will be divided and the buildings sold, to fund the workings of Parliament.'

'And what about his wife?' Kate straightened her back, narrowed her eyes, 'What of her?' Something about her intent manner told me she did not intend to give up her land without a fight.

'A Royalist wife would have no place here,' Downall said.

Kate was quick to retort, 'Royalist or not, at the moment this wife stands for her husband, and will rule in this house.' She drew herself up taller. 'Be so good as to leave us now, Mr Downall. We no longer need your assistance.' It was a slight, and I saw Downall's expression turn grim, but Mallinson nodded at him, and he skulked reluctantly out of the door. When he had gone it was as if the whole room exhaled.

I kept my mouth shut. I secretly hoped the committee would turn Thomas Fanshawe down, for how could there be a future for me with Kate, if her husband was to return?

'Constable Mallinson, what can we do to ensure the Fanshawes retain their rights to the land?' Kate asked, tapping her fingers impatiently on her knee. Oh Lord. I was right.

'Nothing certain,' Mallinson answered. 'There is such a tower of correspondence from Cromwell over the conditions and exceptions. God's eyes, it might take months to wade through it all.' He looked to his son, 'Jacob is helping me, but still, it's a mound of work, and haven't I got enough to do already?' He sighed. 'I'm sorry, but we cannot make any guarantees. Your husband needs to sign a number of different agreements – and there is still the vexing question of whether Parliament owns the farm tenancies—'

'The tenant farmers? Are they not secure?' I could not be quiet, knowing my own livelihood was at stake.

'There's no reason why the tenants should not remain. Though there will be inspections to make sure they are suitable – that they support Puritan values and the new regime.'

'Who will be making these inspections?' I asked, already fearing the answer.

'On this estate? Jack Downall.'

CHAPTER NINE

In Remembrance

For a few days Cutch and I kept out of everyone's way, tilling the land in the scorching heat. I had no heart for anything. I thought of Kate all the time, wondered whether she ached as I did. But she did not approach us, so I had no way of knowing. We had not spoken alone since our argument about the Diggers. Twice a boy came from the town with letters, and I wondered if they were instructions from Cromwell now that the King had fled, or letters from Thomas to Kate. I did not like the thought of him writing to her. But nobody came to tell us anything, so I just carried on, with a great hole in my chest, as though someone had unearthed a boulder there.

I watched Downall and his men from a distance, crawling over the land like locusts, as they inspected the tenants' cottages. Mother told me they had been there the previous night, asking leading questions about their allegiance to Cromwell or the Crown. Mother had given them short shrift, told them her husband died for the Lord Protector, and surely that was good enough?

On Sunday we left from Mother's house for church where we were to give thanks for the lives lost in the recent troubles. The pews were packed with weeping women, the sun shining onto their black-clad shoulders; the church stifling with the smell of wool and sweat. We spotted Abigail near the front, and went to join her. Cutch shuffled in, his hat in his hands, and sat next to me and Mother. I scanned the congregation, but saw no sign of Elizabeth.

At the side of the church in the Fanshawe box, I could see Kate in profile, her head bowed. She glanced my way, and when she saw me watching her she snapped her head back. Even from here, it was as if invisible lightning crackled between us. I couldn't get over the fact she had betrayed me, ridiculed my ideals.

Abigail was peering down the pews, and at the front, I saw Jacob's head turn to give her a smile and mouth, 'later'. She nodded vigorously, and tried not to look too pleased. Constable Mallinson, who was next to Jacob, turned and frowned at us, and cupped his hand to whisper something in Jacob's ear.

When the parson read out the list of names of the deceased, my mother gripped my hand tight. So many men, names I'd known since childhood. Henson the baker, Enwright the cobbler, Mr Johnson the ostler at the Three Tuns. Mother's shoulders heaved with sobs as Father's name was read out. I squeezed her hand but she withdrew it to dab at her eyes. A movement alerted us to the fact that Cutch was crying too. His cheeks were wet and he was scraping away the tears with his sleeve. Mother stared at him a moment as if she'd only just registered his existence, then she handed him a kerchief, empathy softening her expression.

The prayers were long, and my knees numb with kneeling before it was over. Those near the front of the church stood to go, and Kate was one of the first to leave. She darted a look my way, and smiled to Abigail and my mother, but I studiously ignored her. When she'd gone I let out my breath and wished my heart did not pain me so much.

Outside the church a knot of people had gathered to give thanks to the parson and to express their sympathies to each other.

I heard Mother say to Cutch, 'Did you know my husband well?' and Cutch's reply, 'I would not be here at all, were it not for him.'

'Tell me,' she said. And he offered her his arm.

She paused only an instant, before slipping her elbow in his. I watched them walk away together down the path.

'Abigail—' I touched her shoulder to get her attention. I wanted to talk to her about Kate. But Abigail paid me no attention. Her eyes were fixed on Jacob Mallinson and his father who were arguing in low tones over by the graveyard wall. We watched as Constable Mallinson threw us a sidelong look and then tried to persuade Jacob to leave.

Jacob turned his back on his father and strode over, a worried look on his face. His father slapped his riding crop on his thigh in annoyance and was soon trotting away.

'Something's wrong,' Abigail said, when Jacob arrived.

'It's nothing.'

'Yes it is,' Abigail said. 'It's about me, isn't it? I read his lips.'

Jacob sighed. 'He thinks we're not a suitable match. He doesn't want me to see you again.'

'Why? What's he got against Abigail?' I asked. 'Aren't the Chaplins good enough for him?' He'd struck a nerve, and my anger was quick to rise.

'Calm down Ralph. No, it's not that.'

Abigail was watching him with a resigned expression. Her shoulders slumped, the light in her eyes died. 'It's because I'm deaf.' Her mouth trembled. 'I'm right aren't I?'

'I told him, tried to reason with him, but he thinks it a curse,' he turned to me, 'he thinks it a sign that God does not favour her. He's adamant. I tried all last night to change his mind, but he'd have none of it.'

'Your father's right.' Abigail said, two spots of red on her white cheeks. 'I would not want to bring you down.'

'Bring me down? Don't be foolish.' Jacob took hold of both her hands. 'Of course you would not bring me down!'

'We'll call on your father,' I said. 'Make him see sense. If he could get to know Abigail a little better, then he'd see how little difference it makes.'

'What if he won't receive me?' Abi brushed her cheek with her sleeve, where a stray tear had trickled down.

Jacob cupped her face, and wiped the tear gently away with his fingertips. 'Hush. I'm not giving up yet. Ralph's right, if you could persuade your mother to come with us... she's a gentlewoman, and might reassure my father of your good background, add weight to our cause. Do you think she might be willing?'

'I can ask her, and I'm sure she'll say yes. It's just that, the news has only just come about my father, and it wouldn't be seemly for her to be seen to be socialising so soon.'

'Oh.' Jacob was crestfallen. 'Of course. I'm so very sorry. Maybe we should wait...'

'No, I couldn't bear to wait,' Abigail said. 'I'll go and talk to her tonight.'

'And Ralph...?'

'Yes?'

'Like most of the villagers, Downall's fallen on hard times, and my father's trying to help him. They are old friends. It won't help our cause if you make an enemy of him.'

'What do you mean?'

'It's all round the village that you had a fight with Downall at the Manor. Stay away from him. My father grew up with him, and they go back a long way. For my sake and Abi's sake, just keep away from him.'

At that moment the Fanshawes' carriage drew up beside us, and the coachman opened the door for Abigail. I caught a glimpse of Kate's unhappy face before she turned to look out of the other window.

'I must go,' Abigail said.

Jacob kissed her hand. 'I'll see you on your day off on Thursday. Noon at the market cross.'

'I'll be there.'

In one swift movement Jacob pulled her to him and hugged her hard. 'Keep safe.'

Abigail was reluctant to leave, her eyes were fixed on Jacob as she climbed in next to Kate. But the coachman applied his whip and the horses trotted off.

Jacob stared after it until the noise of the wheels died away.

'Will you be able to persuade your father, do you think?' I asked.

He sat down heavily on the wall. 'I don't know. He says he'll cut me off, that he'll stop paying my mercer's apprenticeship if I carry on. And my mother backs him up. She thinks a deaf girl will be no good for my business, and wouldn't be able to manage as a Constable's wife. It would be a meagre marriage without their blessing, and my father's stubborn as hell.'

'You'd better persuade him then. Because it's all your fault. You've led her on. And you'd better not hurt her, or you'll regret it.'

'Don't be like that with me. What's the matter with you? You're angry as a bear over something, and I can't stomach it. I've said, I'll talk to my father.'

And with that, he strode away.

The marriage of a Chaplin girl to the Mallinsons could only improve our family fortunes, yet something in me resisted the dealings with dowry and coin it would entail. Abigail was right, women should not be valued in coin. I thought regretfully of Winstanley and his Diggers pamphlets, and bemoaned the fact that so few thought the way we did.

I hoped Mother would not get too excited on hearing marriage plans were in the air. Not only were Jacob's parents against it, but the other stone in the shoe was Elizabeth. What a weasel she was, plotting to sweet-talk Jacob. Poor Abigail, did she not have problems enough, without a scheming sister like Elizabeth to add to them all?

CHAPTER TEN

The Matchmakers

Two days later I pounded the iron knocker on Constable Mallinson's substantial oak door. Mother and Abigail stood nervously to one side, with Abigail frowning at my boots which were thick with farm dust and needed cleaning.

Jacob opened the door, smart in snowy white shirt and doeskin breeches. He smiled reassuringly at Abigail, 'Come in, come in!'

Abigail stood aside to let Mother and I go in first over the polished stone step. Mother looked thin in the customary black mourning dress, with her hair covered with a black linen coif which made her face appear even more grey and wan than usual. Abigail pressed her lips together in worry. Jacob led us indoors to where his parents stood waiting in the parlour, before a blazing fire. They were dressed in what were obviously their finest clothes, starched and pressed to perfection. The heat was oppressive, and the fire completely unnecessary in summer, but I knew it was designed to give the impression they had money to burn.

With frustration, I saw it was working. My mother was visibly shrinking further into herself, at the sight of them. 'Come on, Mother,' I said in bracing tones, leading her by the arm.

Where was the commanding woman who used to entertain wealthy gentlemen in our fine house? But I knew the answer. That woman had been vanquished by fire, and war and widowhood.

I caught Abigail's eye, gave her a half-smile. I could almost see her thoughts, that Mother did not look very impressive next to the solid, plumpness of Mrs Mallinson, and that I looked like what I was – a tenant farmer. I bowed, doffed my hat, and wished them a polite good evening.

'This is Mrs Chaplin, Father,' Jacob said. 'And you know Ralph.'

Constable Mallinson's look was enough to let me know he remembered me from my time in his cells, and that it was not a savoury memory.

'Pleased to meet you, and may I express my condolences.' Constable Mallinson made a light bow towards my mother, but did not actually meet her gaze.

'It's quite all right...' Mother tailed off anxiously, seeking Abigail's eyes.

Constable Mallinson indicated where we should sit. He had drawn up three chairs for the ladies next to the fire, but even the roaring blaze was not enough to stem Abigail's anxiety; she had not been properly introduced, and was twisting her hair in her fingers, a flush of red embarrassment staining her neck and cheeks.

Mother had barely had time to spread her skirts on the chair when Constable Mallinson began. 'I know that Jacob's grown fond of Abigail, but we think these matrimonial matters are not to be entered into lightly.'

'No indeed,' Mother said, too quick to agree.

'Jacob will inherit this house, and of course will take on my mercer's business as soon as his apprenticeship is done, in say four years. Isn't that right Jacob?'

'If I pass out well enough,' Jacob said, looking modest.

'Oh you will, you will. He's a hard worker my Jacob. I'm right proud of him.'

'Oh, Father—'

'And it's just like him that he's decided to stand for the constabulary. A chip from the old block.' He smiled fondly at Jacob. 'Though you understand it's not easy. You deal with all manner of felons and wrong-doers in my position.'

I could swear he was meaning me, but I said nothing and tried to look innocent.

'And the wife of a constable is an important position in our community,' Mrs Mallinson said. 'She has to put up with the screams of drunkards coming from the cells next door. Not to mention sharing a roof with murderers and being woken all hours, cooking meals that never get eaten, never knowing where her husband has got to—'

'That will do, Jane.' Mr Mallinson cut her off. 'All told, the mercer's shop and the Constabulary will be a substantial living.'

'A substantial living,' echoed Mrs Mallinson.

'To show gratefulness for the good years to come, we would expect any marriage prospect to bring a dower box to the value of...shall we say twenty five pounds?'

Silence.

I looked at Mother uncomfortably.

It was a sum we could not hope to match, and Abigail's slumped shoulders showed she knew it too.

'It's only half of what he'd expect in a year,' Mrs Mallinson said.

It made me angry. 'I don't see why we should not manage that, in time,' I said, thrusting out my chest.

Mother and Abigail both raised their heads and gawped at me as if I had lost my wits. I blundered on, buoyed by the sudden flicker of hope in Abigail's eyes.

'With Lady Fanshawe's permission I intend to expand my father's land,' I boasted, 'and I aim to grow some of the new crops – the clover and alfafa that the Dutch speak so highly of.'

Constable Mallinson stepped away from the fireplace where he had been leaning on the mantel. 'But surely Jack Downall is in charge up at the Manor? Thomas Fanshawe and I agreed it. What does he think of your new-fangled crops? You can't expect Lady Fanshawe to know anything about it, she's but a chit of a girl.'

'On the contrary. Lady Fanshawe seems to know exactly what she is doing with the estate. And she gave me the impression that Downall's position is only temporary,' I said, knowing full well it was just my own wishful thinking.

Constable Mallinson's eyebrows shot up.

'I've agreed with her - I plan to use a fourfold rotation. This will yield more profit per acre.'

'Fourfold rotation? This isn't some ridiculous Diggers notion is it?'

'I'm sure it's not,' Jacob said, hovering behind Abigail's chair, and anxious to preserve the peace.

I crashed on, 'We could pay you the dowry in instalments—'

'How long?' Constable Mallinson interrupted.

'Five years.'

It was a rash promise I had no idea if I could keep, but it silenced Constable Mallinson.

He pursed his lips, went back to the mantel to fill his pipe. Jacob and I sat ourselves down on the settle under the window, but Abigail and my mother stayed motionless on their hard chairs, perspiring in the heat of the fire, whilst Constable Mallinson sucked and spat and puffed, a stubborn set to his lowered brows.

'Two,' he said. 'If you can do it in two then we might be talking.'

'Joseph!' Mrs Mallinson leant over to whisper urgently behind her hand to her husband. 'There's still the issue of her...her...'

'I know, I know,' he hissed, as if we were *all* deaf. 'Leave it to me, woman.'

I saw Abigail's intent gaze on Mrs Mallinson's lips as she pressed him, 'Ask her. Ask her, will she be able to do everything a proper wife should?'

Constable Mallinson rubbed his hand over his mouth. 'The matter is a little delicate...it concerns children...we wondered if any future children might be born with...with...'

'Will they be deaf?' Abigail asked. 'Of course not. I lost my hearing after an illness.'

'Oh.' Mrs Mallinson looked to Jacob. 'Is that right dear? Only when I was talking to her sister in the apothecary's, she gave the impression Abigail was deaf since birth, that she—'

I could not be silent. 'Don't listen to anything Elizabeth says! She said that deliberately to mislead you. She's a liar and—'

'Ralph!' My mother's warning made me bite off my words. But it was too late. Mr and Mrs Mallinson were looking at each other dubiously. By denouncing my sister as an inveterate liar I had only added one more nail to our family coffin.

'Refreshment. Nobody has offered you refreshment.' Jacob stood, a desperate expression on his face.

'Perhaps you misunderstood Elizabeth somehow.' Mother said nervously. 'And we're not here to talk about her. She will easily find someone...I mean, I just wanted to say that Abigail is the sweetest-natured, bravest girl you could imagine.'

'It seems a hard lesson that God is giving her, then.' Mrs Mallinson lifted her nose.

Mother ignored the implication. 'Such a terrible thing to happen to her, yet she manages to do everything any normal young woman could. She can lip-read so well, half the time you'd never know. And she can even write and calculate too, just like anyone. She'd work hard. And she thinks the world of Jacob. She just needs to be given a chance. I have a ring here that was my grandmother's, I'm sure I could part with it...'

Mother twisted the gold band on her finger, trying to remove it.

Abigail's face flared scarlet and humiliation burned in her eyes. 'Don't, Mother.' She stood up, turned to Constable Mallinson. 'You have made your conditions clear. My brother has agreed to furnish the dowry, but I know you might need more time to decide over the other...difficulties.'

She gave me a look that I understood perfectly, and I leapt to my feet. 'We must not keep you from your business,' I said.

Mother stood too, looking a little confused. 'You'll let us know then, will you?'

But Abigail was already walking out of the door. I grasped Mother firmly by the arm, bade a tight good night to the Mallinsons and followed Abigail out.

'Abi, wait.' Jacob came running after us.

But by the time he caught us up in the darkening gloom, Abi was sobbing and would not speak to him.

'What's wrong?' Jacob asked, catching her by the shoulders. 'They'll come round.'

'I can't bear it. All of you discussing me like I'm ... some sort of simpleton! Mother saying I can do things 'normal' girls can, as if I'm not, as if...as if a deaf girl is worth less than everyone else!' She broke away from Jacob's hands. 'I won't be bartered over and sold like I'm a cheap piece of cloth.'

'Hush now, Ralph's said he will find the dowry and—'

'He can't. Ralph and his grand ideas. They never come to anything. You know as well as I do that he's never had a head for business. Money just slips through his hands like water. No wonder he wants to do away with money altogether with his stupid Diggers community.'

They were words said in heat and anger, but they stung me just the same.

CHAPTER ELEVEN

Broken Bones

Cutch and I were up early as the pale sun peeped over the horizon. My mother, who had gone to fetch milk for William, seemed to have warmed to Cutch and had left us home-baked bread and cheese on the table.

I whipped a clean cloth from the drying rail to wrap our provisions. I was anxious to get up the Manor, keen to prove to Abigail and Jacob that my plot would soon be productive and the best tended of them all. Abigail's words had hurt me. I'd always thought my younger sister looked up to me. Was I really the feckless person she'd described? I'd show them.

I tucked the ends of the cloth round the bread remembering how I'd gone straight to Mallinson's shop the very next day, and agreed with Mallinson to provide a dowry for Abigail. Two years – it was agreed. We'd shaken hands and I'd felt his florid damp palm in mine. I'd get that money sooner if I could - and prove them all wrong. They'd all eat their words when I handed over that big fat dowry.

And if it meant putting my own ambitions on hold, and waiting a few years before I could make a Diggers life, then so be it. Abigail might not get another chance, and she was cow-eyed over Jacob. Lord knows why, he seemed pretty ordinary to me. But I was soft, I realised, at least as far as my younger sister was concerned.

I'd had yet another sleepless night, and decided I must try to talk to Kate again. No doubt she would be pleased I'd given up my plans. Though it was only temporary, I told myself. Just till Abigail was wed.

I'd choose a civilised hour to call on Kate. The thought of her gave me a shiver of apprehension.

But as the Manor came into view, I was taken aback to see that the villagers were at work even earlier than we were, and several wagons with big Percheron horses were already ahead of us on the drive. What was more, two other carts passed us on their way to the village, loaded down with sheaves of corn.

When a third came, I waved it down, and was disgruntled to find the shifty eyes of Bill Archer, the miller, staring at me.

'What's happening?' I asked him, surveying the heap of sheaves on the cart.

'It's going to the mill for threshing and grinding,' he said. 'They'll get it back as flour and chaff. Or at least, their share of it.'

'Their share? Surely it all belongs to Lady Fanshawe.'

'Not now it doesn't,' Archer said with relish. He clicked the horse on, and we stood back out of the way.

'It's not right,' I said.

'Thought you were all for sharing it,' Cutch said. 'Isn't that the Diggers way?'

I frowned, although more uncertainly now, and as we watched, another laden cart went by, this time filled with baskets of apples.

The scorching summer had made the trees fruit early. I had seen windfall apples and plums in Kate's orchards, and meant to tell her to begin plucking and preserving them. Now they were disappearing in front of our eyes.

'That fruit–' I asked a woman in a large straw hat, who was sitting on the back of the cart. 'Where's it going?'

'Soper's barn.' she said. 'Come tonight if you want your fair share.'

'Wait!'

But the cart was already creaking its way out of the gates. I turned to Cutch, 'I'm going to see what's going on.'

'Don't you think it would be better to keep out of it?' Cutch said.

I was already on the move though, and when I glanced over my shoulder I saw Cutch shake his head, but then shove his fork into the ground and run after me. When we got to the orchard, we could only stare.

Every tree was stripped bare. Not a single apple, pear or plum remained. The grass was trampled flat round all the trees as if a Biblical horde of locusts had been there.

'Told you so.' I threw the words at Cutch as I strode to the back door and hammered fit to wake the dead.

Abigail stuck her head out of the door. 'What's the matter?'

'Fetch Kate,' I said.

One look at my face was enough to send her scurrying, and a few moments later Kate, hair still mussed from sleep, and roughly dressed in a skirt over her chemise, was following me to the orchard. I told her what I'd seen.

Her eyes travelled over the denuded trees, with an expression of disbelief. 'They won't get away with it.'

We found Downall in the yard. 'What do you mean, taking all our corn and all our fruit?' Kate said, 'Who gave you permission to do that?'

Downall smiled long and slow. 'Why you did, Milady.'

'I did not.'

'You were glad enough to get your harvest in. And how else will you pay folk? You'll get your share like everyone else. Except that seeing as you haven't worked for it, your share will be less.'

'But it is my land and my crop!'

'I heard tell you were a Digger. Soper says he heard tell you were with them that built on the common.' He gave a wily grin, 'So you believe in the earth belonging to all, don't you?'

'But this isn't fair! You're stealing my harvest. What will I sell, how will I—'

'Tis too late, now anyway,' Downall said. 'It's gone to Soper's barn.'

'We'll see about that.' I shouted, setting off after Kate, who was already running into the yard.

The last cart, laden with stooks of barley, was about to leave. Several men were briskly sweeping the yard of the chaff.

Hitching up her skirts Kate leapt onto the tailgate and scrambled aboard. Like a crazy woman she hoisted up sheaf after sheaf and tumbled them one by one back into the yard.

'What are you doing? Get down!' Ned Soper waved his pitchfork at her.

'Kate!' I shouted with him, but she did not heed me, her breath coming in short gasps as she hurled the barley down.

Around me, Ned's workers closed in on the cart, threatening her with their pitchforks, and trying to load the bundles back on. I pushed through, leapt up onto the cart beside her. Ned scrambled up behind us and tried to pinion Kate's arms, but she twisted away, dragged another sheaf to the edge and tipped it over. I gathered up another few and threw them into the yard.

Ned wrenched Kate's arm up her back. 'Leave go,' she cried. 'You'll not take it. It's mine by right!'

The sight of the filthy Ned Soper with his hands on Kate incensed me. 'How dare you!'

I tried to wrestle him away, but he would not let go. I grabbed his fingers and bent them back, forcing his grip to loosen. Kate staggered back away from him. He lurched towards her again to take hold, but I pushed him off with a great shove.

In horror I watched Kate reach out to grab him as he toppled backwards, his arms flailing, grasping at nothing. For a moment his body hung in mid-air, his mouth open in shock. A thud and a crunch. The gasp from the onlookers, told me he had hit the ground. Men rushed forwards to look.

I jumped down, tried to part the sea of bodies, but they were all stepping back to make a circle. In the centre, Ned Soper did not move; his legs were bent at an odd angle, the pimples on his face red against the white.

I looked up. Kate was still standing on the cart, a sheaf in her arms, but she was motionless, as if she held her breath.

A white cap amongst the crowd, pushing through. Abigail.

'What's going on?' she signed.

'It's Ned,' I pointed, mimed 'tumbling' with my hands..

'An accident. He fell off the cart.' Kate said.

John Soper crouched over his son. 'Pushed, more like,' he said. 'Speak to me, Ned, where does it hurt?'

Ned uttered another groan of pain and his lips were grey as goose grease. He turned on his side and retched.

'Help him somebody!' John Soper said, tugging at his arm. 'We need to get him up.'

'No, don't move him yet,' Abigail said, 'give him room.' The crowd moved back a little.

'Is he alright?' Kate said, suddenly all motion, scrambling down.

I put my hand out to help her. Her face was almost as pale as Ned Soper's. I squeezed her arm, but she did not meet my eyes.

My stomach churned, 'It was an accident,' I repeated. 'He overbalanced. Cutch!' I called, my voice full of panic.

The people parted to let Cutch through. He crouched to feel Ned's arm. More yells of pain.

'Cutch will know what's wrong,' I told Soper. 'Seen every type of break on the battlefield. If something's broken, he'll likely be able to fix it.'

'Hope he's better at fixing bones than cartwheels,' someone muttered.

'It's your fault. I'll not pay a bone-setter's fee,' Soper grumbled.

'I'll do it gratis,' Cutch said, running practised fingers over Ned's shirt. 'It's broken right enough. Shoulder's smashed.'

My heart seemed to collapse inwards. Ned was hurt, and it was all my fault. I hated him, and felt sorry for him at the same time.

'Can you fix it?' I shifted awkwardly from foot to foot.

Cutch sucked in his breath. 'Not the shoulder. It's a long job, and not much I can do. But nothing else is broken. He'll have to rest, take liquor to ease the pain.'

'You did it on purpose,' Downall said staring straight at me.

With a supreme effort, I clenched my teeth. It would do Ned no good to argue. We could sort it out later. 'Empty the cart, and give us a hand. We'll see he gets home,' I said.

Downall gave orders for someone to fetch the board from the trestle table in the dairy as a stretcher. Meanwhile Cutch had found a fence lath to make a splint and bind the arm to the body, with much yelling and groaning from Ned.

'What about compensation?' Soper said, glaring at Kate. 'It was your fancy-man pushed him.'

'Don't dare to speak to Lady Fanshawe that way.' I could no longer keep quiet. I appealed to the knot of workers, 'You all saw it. He lost his footing. None of it would have happened at all if you hadn't been stealing—'

John Soper stood up, wagged a finger at me. 'You wait. I'm going to talk to Mallinson. There'll be new laws now Cromwell's in charge. The King's fled. You won't get away with pushing us around, you and your Fanshawe shit.'

'Pa!' More groans from the cart drew Soper reluctantly back to his son.

The cart set off with Ned yelping at every bump in the track. Soper turned and yelled, 'If he can't work, or if it doesn't mend, I swear I'll fleece you bastards for every penny you have.'

'And thank you to you, too,' muttered Cutch. 'Ungrateful bastard.'

I glanced over to Kate and Abigail, who watched the cart's slow progress down the drive with their arms wrapped around each other.

Downall picked up his rake from where he'd dropped it earlier, began to push the sheaves into a pile.

'What do you think you're doing?' I asked.

'Getting back to work,' he said, 'what do you think?' He waved his arm to the crowd who began to drift away.

'Oh no you're not.' I said.

'Ralph,' Abigail's warning voice, 'Please. You've done enough damage.'

'You're not working here, not unless you see to it that every last grain is returned to Lady Fanshawe's barn.' I braced my shoulders, saw Downall's eyes narrow.

The men who were dispersing paused, stared.

'Look at yourself,' Downall sneered, 'What were you fighting for? You don't give a toss for the common man. All that Diggers talk of sharing, but one look from the lady of the manor and you'd lick the King's arse if she told you to—'

My fist shot out, catching Downall on the cheek. It was like hitting a stone wall, but he staggered back, clutching his face.

There was an audible gasp from the farmworkers behind me. Cutch leapt to my side, grabbed my shoulder.

'You shit.' Downall looked at his hand to see if there was blood.

My knuckles stung, and tears sprang up in my eyes. I hadn't meant to do that. God, what was I thinking? I'd already pushed a man off a cart. I dropped my head to my chest. Cutch pulled me closer into a protective huddle.

'I will have respect.' Kate addressed Downall in a voice that was sharp as flint. 'You're dismissed,' she turned to me then, her face suffused with anger, 'Both of you. I won't have fighting here.'

She turned and walked to the back door, her back rigid as a board. The slam of the door made me wince.

In the yard all was silence. Abigail had both hands over her mouth, her eyes brimming with tears. She turned to me, 'You fool. You've ruined everything.' Then she bunched her skirts in her fists, ran after Kate.

Downall kicked his rake to one side. One eye was watering and a bruise was coming already on his cheek. 'You're too free with your fists, Chaplin. Constable Mallinson will hear of this,' he said, 'and when he does, I wouldn't like to be in your shoes.'

CHAPTER TWELVE

The Hunt

At mother's cottage I was up early, unable to sleep. The events of the day before rolled round my head over and over. Everything was going wrong. I knew I should not go near the Manor, but Kate drew me there as if I was bewitched. I prayed to God he'd take away the longing in my heart, but it burned there still.

I put my spade over my shoulder and crept out past Cutch's curled and sleeping shape.

The land had always been my solace, and hard physical work my comfort. I did not know what else to do to ease my heart, but dig. Maybe that was why a Digger's life spoke to me so. In the pale dawn the view was so beautiful, it made me catch my breath, the sight of the deep belt of green oaks beyond the meadow, the heat haze shimmering over the dew. A few orderly stooks of corn marked where the gold had been shaved to a soft brown, and where after yesterday's events, all work had stopped.

I inhaled a deep breath, sighed. I wished it had been me, not Downall, coaxing the land back to its seasonal cycle. The land being worked was the only sign that order might at last return to England. After the King had been beheaded and even his distraught son could not scramble an English army to defend him, it seemed like England herself had lost her head. In the last six months, my life had been turned upside-down by war and my father's death.

But even more so by love.

The very sight of Kate was still enough to set a tremble in my chest. It was as if my eyes were caught to her by a string, wherever she moved I couldn't help but watch. Her grace and strength in equal measure wrung out something deep inside me.

Yet I had to confess, I was no longer certain who or what Kate was. Before I left for Worcester, she had been set on the Diggers ideals of freedom, but in just a few short weeks the tug of her aristocratic past had begun to draw her away from me. How could I compete with all those generations of tradition and power, the sheer weight of her forebears? And now I was weakening too. I was being worn down by the needs of society for dowries and certainties.

I felt as if I was grasping after shadows.

But I would not be defeated. There would be setbacks, perhaps. But I would fight for Kate and for my vision of the future for as long as I had the strength.

I struck my spade deep into the soil until I felt the crunch of it under my boot. Stood on its edge to feel it slice deeper, turned over the rich brown earth. The land in front of me was unchanging. The trees still grew, the river still flowed, despite the wars of men. As if to keep me company, the early blackbird sang its sweet, sharp song.

After I had been digging a while, Cutch arrived and began to work beside me, lifting the earth over with his fork, the clang of iron and the patter of earth the only other sounds. When we heard hoof beats, we looked up, shaded our eyes.

Jacob Mallinson reined in his horse in a skid of earth and stones.

'You fool! I warned you to keep away from Downall,' he shouted without dismounting. 'My father has a warrant for your arrest. Downall's put in a complaint. You hit him, didn't you?'

'I had to. He was stealing, and he insulted Kate.'

Jacob slid down. 'I don't know what it is with you, Ralph, but trouble sticks to you like a burr. Father's angry as hell. I'd just about persuaded him that you really were serious about Abigail's dowry, and then Downall comes to our door looking like he's been in a prize-fight.'

'It wasn't my fault—'

Jacob shook his head. 'That's what you always say. You're a fool, Ralph. You've put the fox right among the pigeons this time. Father's telling me the Chaplins are no match for his son. What shall I tell Abigail? Answer me that?'

His desperate expression cowed me. I scuffed my boot in the dirt, I had never known Jacob so angry.

'I didn't mean to—'

'It's far too late for apologies. They're after your blood. They're saying you deliberately threw Ned Soper off a cart and broke his shoulder—'

'I did not!'

'It was an accident,' Cutch said.

Jacob sighed in annoyance. 'Never mind the ins and outs of it all now, there's no time. You'd best hide out somewhere until it all blows over. Have you somewhere you can go?'

'Only Mother's, and that will be no use, it'll be the first place they'll look. Is there really a warrant out for me?'

'You don't know my father. He sees any disorder in the village as a personal insult, and a slight on his ability to keep the law. He told Downall to get six armed men to come after you and your friend to bring you back to—'

'Oh, grateful thanks, Ralph.' Cutch threw down his fork, 'Now my neck's on the line too.'

Jacob glanced over his shoulder. 'Look, my father would kill me for even being here, But I had to come - I overheard Downall tell his men to shoot if they got within range of you, that they'd not to wait to see if you hand yourselves in.'

'Hellfire,' Cutch said. 'What shall we do?'

'Look, I'm only doing this for Abigail's sake, mind, because I don't want her to have to deal with a dead brother. There's a ruined cottage on the other side of Wheathamstead Wood, a few miles from here. It's the only place I know where they might not look.'

'Is it far?'

'A couple of miles or so, and it's well off the road, hidden in the woods – used to be the charcoal burner's house, but he was lost at the battle of Preston and it's all overgrown. Do you know it? We used to go visit with him when we were boys, remember?'

I nodded.

'Should be safe for a day or two until you think of something else,' Jacob said. 'It's the best I can do.'

'Thanks, friend.' I reached out my hand but Jacob declined to shake it.

'I must have lost my wits,' Jacob said. 'You sure as hell don't deserve it. I'm doing it for Abigail. She's had enough deaths for one year. You'll need horses to stand a chance, though, Downall's men will be close behind me, they were gathering in the square when I left.' Jacob wedged his foot in the stirrup and mounted up. 'Get well away. And once you're out of the county, then you can send Abigail word of where you are.'

With that he cantered away across the field in the other direction, probably anxious not to meet his father on the way home. Cutch hastily gathered all our tools together, one eye on the horizon, and we ran to the Manor yard, but there was nobody about. Perhaps they were all in Downall's party. The thought made my mouth dry.

We hustled our horses from the stables and tacked them up. Cutch vaulted into the saddle, but saw my hesitation. 'What?'

'I can't just go,' I said. 'Not without speaking to Kate.'

Cutch lifted a leg and bent to tighten the girth on his horse. 'You're mad. Those men are armed. Let's get on our way. Time for all that later.'

'A few minutes. Keep a look out, will you?'

I heard him curse, then shout impatiently after me, but I ignored him.

The kitchen door was locked, but I ran round to the main door, and to my surprise, when I tried it, it opened. Kate was standing in the hall. Her eyes were shadowed as if she had not slept, her hair tangled.

'I saw you both come up the drive,' she said, keeping her distance.

'I have to go away,' I said. 'There's a warrant for my arrest.'

'Already? Downall's wasted no time then.'

'They could be on their way now, so I must make haste.'

'So you will run, rather than face it?' her eyes challenged me.

'Please,' I put my hand out to her. 'Don't be like that. You know it's not the first time I've hit someone. My fists seem to have a fury of their own. I fear no sweet words of Jacob's will work to get me out of gaol, even if he tried. And they're armed. Jacob says Downall will shoot to kill.'

I saw the words register and her eyes flash with fear. 'Saints preserve us.' She swayed slightly. 'Where will you go?'

'Best you don't know.' My voice broke, betrayed me. 'Best you forget I came.'

Her eyes were travelling over my face, searching to see how I felt. 'I can't forget a single moment I've spent with you,' she said quietly.

Our eyes locked as I stumbled towards her, clumsily, wanting only to feel her in my arms. Her hands came round my waist, clinging to me as if she could not let me go.

'I love you, Kate.' The relief that she had forgiven me making my heart soar.

'And I you. But it's hopeless.' She was already pulling away. 'Before you go, you must read this.' She pulled a letter from a hanging pouch in her skirts.

'What is it?' I was immediately wary.

'There's no time to explain. Just read it.'

'Dear wife,' it began. So it was from Thomas. I looked up. Her eyes were full of pain.

'Go on,' she said, 'read it. It is best you know.'

'My uncle and I cannot openly return to England. To do so would be to risk being hunted down by Cromwell and his men, and certain death or transportation would result. I have tried to negotiate with the Committee to make peace with Parliament, but so far they have proved less than amenable. As soon as I can arrange a safe passage I will come to fetch you. You will join me in France until the King's fortunes are restored. Shut up the house, sell the furniture and all the livestock while you can. Conceal the gold plate somewhere where we can retrieve it later.

Our time will come again, but meanwhile I ask you to take care of this inheritance, for it will be our children's fortune in years to come. Prepare your travelling trunk with all haste, by the time you receive this I will be on my way. I will come by night, so be ready to make speed away.'

Endearments followed which I could not stomach to read.

'Will you go with him?' I had to know.

'The estate will be broken up anyway, even if I do nothing.' She could hardly speak the words for emotion.

'You didn't write to tell Thomas what happened when the Roundheads came, did you?' I said softly.

'No, there wasn't time.'

I passed the letter back, and she paced away down the empty hall, where the paneling still bore the gouges of Roundhead swords. 'What shall I do?' she asked.

The house itself seemed sad. Grice the overseer had stripped it, then the Roundheads had finished the job. Thomas had not set foot here for more than six months, and no doubt would be shocked to see the state of the house now – his fine furniture gone, the portraits slashed or looted, the gardens overgrown with weeds.

I knew how much Kate loved the house. To be truthful I could not see her anywhere else, but I could not admit that to myself; it opened too many wounds.

Kate turned and came back towards me, the letter swinging limply in her fingers.

'You can't leave,' I said. 'They need you here. Only yesterday you were worried about the tenants. And what about Abigail's position?' I paused, grabbed hold of her hand, 'What about us?'

'Do you think I haven't thought of us?' She was almost angry. 'I think of you every minute of every day. It's like a puzzle maze - full of dead ends, and I can't find my way out.'

'How long have you had the letter?'

'It's no use. I'm just torturing myself. I'm under my husband's command. Thomas is on his way, and if Sir Simon has anything to do with it, my husband will have orders to persuade me to go to France by fair means or foul.'

'Isn't there somewhere you can go where he can't find you?'

'Let me come with you,' she said.

'No. I wish I could say yes, but I can't risk it. They're shooting to kill.'

'Then if Thomas arrives, I'll try to stall him somehow.' Her voice dropped to a whisper, uncertain. 'Ralph...you'll come back, won't you?'

'Of course I will. There'll be a time for us, I promise.'

A piercing whistle from outside. Cutch's warning.

I ran to the window. Outside I saw the faint outlines of a group of horsemen approaching, evidenced by the rolling cloud of dust.

'Is it them?' Kate asked, running over to join me.

'I fear so.'

'Then for God's sake, go.'

I pulled her to me, planted a desperate kiss on her lips, felt her mouth respond to mine and her faint heartbeat against my chest, but she pushed me away.

'Go safe, my love' she entreated.

At the door, I looked back at her, my heart a turmoil of longing, 'I pray God, Thomas's ship sinks,' I said, 'with him on it.'

Outside, Cutch had my horse by the reins. 'Quick,' he shouted. 'Christ in heaven, I thought you were never coming.'

I vaulted astride and shouted, 'Out the back way, across the fields. Head for the church!'

We clattered out of the yard and kicked our horses on across the hard-packed ground. A shout from behind alerted us to the fact we'd been seen. Together we urged our horses faster. Ahead of us, the gate to the next field was open and with the sun in our eyes we headed for the narrow gap.

Cutch pelted through, but I drew to a halt, pushed the gate shut with all my might. Cutch was a blur now on the other side of the field and I galloped after. Shutting the gate had lost me time, but I heard the curses and commotion as the party behind got to the gate. I looked over my shoulder just in time to see Downall level a pistol at me from over the wall. I heard the shot, but did not feel anything. My horse seemed to sense the danger and increased his speed.

A second shot rebounded from a hawthorn tree just to my left, but I galloped on. When I turned to look back, the other party had just made it through the gate. We thundered through the village, our hooves clattering on the stony road, flying past the ale-house and the sheets tentered out to dry on the village green. As soon as we reached the woods we plunged into them, tree branches whipping in our faces. Ahead of me, a low branch took off Cutch's hat.

He slowed, his chest heaving. He was out of breath. 'I'll have to ...fetch it,' he said, 'or they'll see... which way we've gone.'

'No time,' I gasped. 'Just keep going.'

The track divided in several places and we just forged on, our sweating horses more and more reluctant. When we hit a clearing we stopped.

'Which way?' Cutch asked.

I looked behind me. There was no sign of our pursuers.

'Think we lost them,' I said.

We listened, our ears straining for the sound of horsemen breaking through the forest, but there was silence.

'Do you think they've given up?' Cutch wiped his sweating forehead.

'I don't know,' I said. But I somehow doubted it.

CHAPTER THIRTEEN

A Savage Secret

The woods were dense and we were jumpy as hares. It took us several wrong paths before we saw the charcoal burner's house, because we were searching for the coppiced wood, the places where the undergrowth was thinnest, reckoning that the man would have done the most work nearest to his house. In fact, the cottage was almost overgrown, and there was no sign anyone had been here for years.

'Well I wouldn't exactly call it shelter,' Cutch said, eyeing the crumbling wattle and daub walls, and the holes in the thatch.

But it felt better than being out in the open, even in this ramshackle place. We would have a place to defend, at least, if it came to that. 'And look – a trough, I said. 'He must have had a horse.'

There was a few inches of greenish water in the bottom, so we let the horses drink.

'What about us? Don't like the stink of that water,' Cutch said.

'There's a stream about a half mile from here. One of us will have to go and fetch water, then say our prayers, because we can't brew it.'

We brought the horses over the threshold, out of sight.

Neither of us could sleep. We were hungry, and too much on edge. Every noise of pheasant or partridge made my heart pound. Twice we leapt up at sounds in the forest. 'Deer,' Cutch said.

The next day we set snares for rabbit, and dug a fire pit. We knew we would have to survive by our wits and could not risk going into the villages. We rethatched the roof with bracken and twigs for something to do, and because that way we did not think of our empty stomachs.

Cutch found the stream about a half mile away, and filled water flagons.

'See anything?' I asked, when he returned.

'Nothing. No sign of anyone at all. But there was a wild apple tree, so I filled my pockets with apples, and blackberries.'

He tossed me a wormy apple, and we crunched our way through the lot. The blackberries were still red and sour, but the apples made me think of Kate's harvest. I daren't think about her. I feared she would be forced into exile in France. Would I ever see her again?

Cutch picked up on my morose attitude and kept me busy building a fire pit. We would need to cook meat if we were to survive without the markets of the villages. Apart from our weapons, we only had our horses, our bundles of clothes and the tools that had been already in the saddlebags. Cutch had grabbed bows and quivers from the hooks in the stable, and with these we hoped to hunt boar or deer. We waited till dark to cook, and hoped no-one would see our smoke.

'You made a decent job of that roof,' Cutch said, as we sat roasting a rabbit.

'Living with the Diggers was a good training. They burnt our houses that many times we got used to thatching.'

He laughed, tore off some meat with his teeth. 'Were you really a Digger? I thought they were all madmen.'

'Well I'm one of them, so maybe you're right. They were good people. But it was like a mouse fighting a pack of dogs. We just couldn't survive. Too few of us. And hard, if you have to be so holy.'

'What do you mean?'

'We couldn't fight back. The leader, Winstanley, was against it. He wanted peaceful protests. But there has to be a difference between just letting yourself be bullied and making a stand.'

Cutch gave me a pointed look. 'You seem to make a habit of making a stand. You keep thumping people.'

I put down the rabbit bone I'd been holding. 'I never intend to. It's just when I get angry my fists speak instead of my tongue.'

'Why, Ralph? What is it that eats you?'

'I don't know. Guess my father was like that when he'd had a bellyful of ale. He used to hit out when he'd had a few. And he couldn't bear it if you didn't follow his orders.'

'Aye, he was like that on the battlefield right enough. But it was a good thing. He had control over his men.'

'He shot a horse once because it would not obey.'

'A horse?'

'He wanted it to jump a ditch but it kept refusing. He shouted and bellowed, got it in a right lather. 'You're no use to me,' he screamed at it, and by the end he lost his wits, he got so red with rage that he jumped down and put a musket ball between its eyes. I couldn't do anything to save it, the beast just crumpled before my eyes, its flanks still steaming. I've never forgotten it. It filled me with a kind of horror, that such a small ball could fell such a big horse.'

'Gawd. Poor horse.'

'I think I'm still angry at him.'

'About the horse?'

'No. Not just the horse. Everything. The way we all had to knuckle under to his orders. Useless though, to talk of him, now he's dead.'

A sudden screech. We froze a moment listening, but it was just a hunting owl. It flew low over our heads like a pale shadow.

'Makes sense that.' Cutch wiped his greasy hands on the seat of his pants. 'I've never said nothing – didn't seem right, but when we were in Maidstone a few years ago, your father was defending an uprising against Cromwell over celebrating Christmas. But it was like you said, he just lost his reason.'

I waited, watched him swallow before he could say more.

'Folks wanted the day off, and to put up their holly trees and suchlike, like they used to in the season. Well, Cromwell had ordered us to take the trees down – pagan idols, he called it. But then the Copthornes from the Big House kept encouraging folks to put them up, and before long it grew into a riot, with the Copthorne family egging everyone on to sing songs and feast in the open air.'

'The Copthornes? That name's familiar.'

'You slayed one of them at Worcester. The elder brother, Philip. But this is about his father, Lord Sydney Copthorne.'

The face of the other brother, Edward, pricked at my memory. 'What of them? What have they to do with my father?'

'Your father and I were part of the troop ordered to quash the Christmas celebration. I was in the square burning the holly, when Lord Copthorne challenged me. I tried to run off, but he caught up with me and was just about to slit my throat, when your father came. He was in one of his rages and chased Copthorne off. Your father saved my life.'

'Then I'm glad I got his son in the end.'

Cutch shifted on the log he was sitting on, shook his head. 'No. That's not all.'

'Go on.'

'The next day, there was another skirmish. Your father was drunk again and Lord Copthorne had seen your father struggle to mount his horse. Copthorne shouted insults across the lines, told him he was too drunk to fight properly, made fun of him in front of his men, taunted him. Called him a drunken sot and Lord knows what else.'

Cutch paused, picked at a bit of grass near his feet. 'But we were victorious that day, we quashed the

Royalist uprising. But your father was not satisfied. I've never seen a man so angry. He took a troop of horsemen and ...'

'What?'

'He shot the whole family.'

I was silent. Waited for more.

'He asked for directions to Lord Copthorne's house, the Big House. He armed his men, had them break in and round up the whole family. He ordered us to bring them into the yard in their nightclothes. Children, women. Then he took his pistol and shot each one. They had nowhere to run. He took the pistols off his men, so he could fire each shot. He took mine to shoot the youngest. Must have been only about four years old. That boy had such a look of puzzlement on his face.'

'What did you do?'

'Nobody survived it, only the two elder Copthorne brothers who had been playing in the hayloft above the stables. Philip and Edward. We heard later that they saw it all.'

Copthorne's frenzied slaying of my father suddenly made sense. 'Go on,' I said.

'No. I don't think I—'

'Tell me, damn you. I need to know.'

'I couldn't hold that gun no more. I threw it away. That night your father fell asleep in his tent as usual. His snores made us uncomfortable; that he could sleep so sound. Those of us that had been there could not meet each other's eyes. We'd witnessed something we didn't want to remember. In the morning I asked your father if he remembered the night before. 'No idea,' he said. Can you believe it, afterwards he could not remember any of it. I couldn't help thinking of those two young boys watching from the stables. Christmastide, and no-one to make merry with, their family rotting in the yard.'

My heart twisted. My father had done that. I couldn't grasp it. 'Did you hate him?'

'No. He saved my life. In a sword fight against a cavalier. But he was a different man when the drink was on him - angry, dark, bitter. Then it was best to keep out of his way.'

'You say he shot all these people?'

'We were at war, Ralph. I keep telling myself, odd things happen in war. Savage things. We turn from men into beasts. You have to forgive and forget, or you'd turn bedlam.'

'That explains why Edward Copthorne said he'd hunt me down. I thought he was just crazed.'

Cutch paused, raised his eyebrows and gave me his full attention. 'He said that?'

'After I killed his brother. What he said to me made no sort of sense at the time, but it does now.'

Cutch crossed himself. 'God preserve us all. Edward Copthorne's the last of his line. I've seen him fight, you know. He's got more than a touch of your father about him, himself. Ruthless. Too much war, I'll wager; it sours you if you're not careful.'

'Do you think Copthorne'll come after me?'

Cutch evaded my question. 'He's probably been arrested or transported by now,' he said carefully. 'Better worry about Downall and his men instead. They're closer to home. Come on, if you've finished eating we'd best bury this fire before someone sees it.'

We threw the bones of the rabbit into the fire and kicked earth over the pit. When I'd done I stood a moment, looking at the smoking ground. It reminded me of the heat haze shimmering over the corpses in the field where my father died.

I turned to Cutch. 'I've tried to forget it, you know. Worcester I mean. But it haunts me, like it's eaten deep inside me, the sight of those men lying on the field. Carrion crows pecking at their unseeing eyes. And all I could think of, was their womenfolk sitting waiting at home, still darning their hose, all unawares.'

'Aye, I hope there's an end of war between Englishmen.' Cutch spat out a bone, helped me stamp the earth flat. We stamped harder and longer than was necessary.

'Shall I re-set the snares?'

'If you like. This rabbit's been tasty enough, but we'll soon tire of it. If we're staying here any length of time we'll need bread, grain for brewing, warm clothing when the cold sets in, and something to trade. We sure as eggs can't live the Diggers way, not if we're going to survive here.'

'It might only be a few more days.'

Cutch gave a curt laugh. 'Didn't sound like they'd forget you that quick. Months might be more like.'

'Fatalist.'

'We'll still need supplies though. A whetstone for sharpening. Soap. A cooking pot or two would be nice. And I fancy a new pair of breeches.'

'What?'

He grinned. 'Only joking.'

I pushed him on the shoulder. 'I thought you liked living rough.'

'There's rough... and then, there's this.'

'Oh milady! Didn't know you were so fussy. We'll soon be out of here.'

'Guess we'll spend a few days here, then go North. Out of this county, where Downall and his men can't reach us.'

I sat down heavily on a tree stump. My stomach clenched. 'I can't.'

'But you just said—'

'I know what I said. But I can't leave Kate.' I put my head in my hands. 'What a mess.'

'She's a married woman, Ralph. Married to Thomas Fanshawe. What good will it do, hanging round here? You'll just torture yourself.'

'There's Abigail and my mother. I'm supposed to be taking care of them. I promised Abigail her dowry. And I can't leave Kate. Cromwell's men won't be kind to Royalist women. What if she needs me?'

Cutch sighed in frustration. 'It's none of your business. Let her husband look to her. You know I'm right. You have to forget her, Ralph.'

'I can't. Don't ask me why, but I can't.'

CHAPTER FOURTEEN

A Night Visitor

A crack of a twig woke me, and I felt through the darkness for Cutch's sleeping form and shook him by the shoulder. 'Visitors,' I whispered.

He was on his feet in moments fumbling for his sword. There was no time to load a pistol, and we had no fire to light firepowder anyway. The soft crackle of leaves and beechnuts underfoot was closer now.

I took my sword and stood behind the doorway, Cutch readied himself by the window, ready to leap out. We peered into the blackness but could see nothing. Silence enveloped us. Then the noise again, very close now. A single person by the sound of it. Downall. Just outside the door. I leapt out, sword in hand.

A scream as my hand went around the throat.

It was a woman. Her cloak and skirts brushed against my knees.

'Let go!'

'Abigail! You fool. I nearly killed you.' I took her hand, traced the sign for 'the middle of the night' on her palm, made a face.

'It was the only time I could come. Downall's back on the estate, and he's watching us both to see if we make contact with you.'

'You weren't followed?' She did not understand. 'Come.' I pulled her inside, where Cutch had lit a lantern. We sat round its meagre light, so Abigail could read our faces.

'Nobody saw you come?' I asked again.

She shook her head, wrapped her cloak tighter. 'Of course not. Jacob told me where he'd sent you. I came to see if you'd gone.'

'You shouldn't have come out in the dark. You're all a-shiver.'

'I can't stay long. Did you know Sir Thomas arrived last night? He came in the small hours.'

'Sir Simon wasn't with him?'

'No, just a small retinue of servants.'

My stomach dropped. Already.

'He was horrified at the state of the house and grounds and rode over to talk to Constable Mallinson about the lawlessness in his absence, and whether he could regain any of his lost goods. After initial disagreements, apparently they were reconciled, so long as he agreed Downall would continue to manage the estate. Kate was furious about Downall, but there was little she could do, now the Master of the house is home.'

'Is Sir Thomas trying to persuade Kate to go with him, back to France?'

'Not any more. Constable Mallinson said that it would be better if he could be seen to be doing his best for the village – that way he might be able to persuade the Committee to let him keep his lands. They've struck some sort of bargain. Now the King is out of the country, they just want things to get back to normal as soon as possible. Mallinson will put in a word for him with Cromwell's new regime, if he employs certain people in the village. So no, I think Thomas is going to try and stay. He's grown up – he's more sure of himself. He wants to rid himself of his uncle's rule, and do things his own way.'

I wasn't sure if this was worse news or better news. I tried to weigh up the implications. One thing was certain though, while ever he was there I would not be welcome at Markyate Manor, and it would make it nigh on impossible to get near to Kate.

'It's good news. I was dreading France,' Abigail went on, 'I would have had to go with her, and I couldn't bear it. To be amongst strangers again. It takes me so long to get familiar, so I can read their lips. And I couldn't manage another language, I just know I couldn't. English is hard enough.'

'So now he's back, what is his precious Lordship going to do?' I said scathingly.

Abigail frowned. 'Unlike *some*, he wants to mend the rifts in our neighbourhood, not stir up trouble.'

'Hey, I wasn't—'

'For heaven's sake, Ralph, I'm your sister. Don't try to fool me. At least it means Downall will be too busy kow-towing to Thomas Fanshawe to waste time searching for you.' She stood again, brushed the bracken off her skirt, leant her back against the wall.

Cutch caught her eye. 'How's your mother?'

'Distraught of course. Worried to death about Ralph. Wondering how she'll manage with no man's wage. Downall has put the word out that if you show your faces again, you're to be arrested. There's notices up with your descriptions in Wheathamstead, St Albans... all the villages nearby.'

Cutch looked to me, it was not what we wanted to hear.

'Ralph,' burst out Abigail, 'Please, stay away. Go to some other town, find work there. You'll be safer, and when this has all blown over, I'll write to you and you can come home. I need to keep my work at the Manor, and if you cause any more trouble there,

Thomas Fanshawe will see that I'll lose it. And then what would Mother do?'

'You're telling me to get out of your life? Your own brother?'

She stood. 'It's not like that, you know it's not. It's just...it would be best if you went away for a while.'

'I can't.'

Abigail turned to Cutch. 'It's Kate, isn't it?'

Cutch nodded.

She sighed. 'Please, Cutch, you've got to help me to persuade him. We just want peace. And Jacob's father won't consider me, not whilst Ralph is still an outlaw on his patch.'

So my feelings didn't matter. It was all about her and Jacob.

'What does Kate think?' I asked. 'You haven't told me what she thinks.'

'She's pleased.' Abigail looked at me defiantly. 'The master has told her he will rebuild the house. Make it a grand house again, like it was in her mother's day. That he'll re-furnish it and restore it to life. And when he came back from meeting Constable Mallinson,' she said, 'he'd brought a beautiful glass vase, found it at the market. It used to be the one that sat on the dining table, before Grice and the Roundheads came. Thomas had filled it with full-blown roses from the garden. I've never seen Kate's face so raw with pain. It brought her to tears.'

I turned away. The needle in my chest was so sharp I could hardly breathe.

'I know it's not what you wanted to hear, but better for you to know how things are.'

'A few roses won't make any difference to Kate,' I said.

Abigail read my feelings in my face, but I saw her harden her expression. 'Sorry Ralph, but I have to go. Nobody knows I'm here. I wheedled your whereabouts from Jacob, but Kate thinks I'm sleeping, and I need to be back in time for my early morning duties if the master is not to dismiss me.'

'The master,' I said. 'S'truth, it's 'the master' now.'

Abigail reached out to touch me but I shrugged her off.

'Try to persuade him,' she said softly to Cutch.

'If you'll permit me, Miss Abigail, I'll bring the lantern and walk with you a mile or two until you're safe on the road,' Cutch said.

'Thanking you,' Abigail said. I heard the relief in her voice. I knew she found darkness difficult.

A few moments later and I was the one alone in the darkness with just my thoughts. The silence closed round me like a shroud.

What was it all for?

All that fighting, and Thomas Fanshawe was going to walk back in to his house and be the lord of the manor just as before. And Kate. I never thought I cared a fig for luxuries, that they were irrelevant. But now I cared about having them. Not for myself, but for Kate. It should have been me bringing her roses in a glass vase.

I had never thought of myself as jealous, but the thought of Thomas buying gifts for Kate made me want to smash something. Women loved fine silks and beautiful surroundings, and it hurt me that I would never be able to provide them, that Kate would always need to look to someone else. Someone rich like the Fanshawes, not a poor farmer like me. It made me feel less like a man, that I could not give her what she needed. Prosperity showed the world you were someone. What was I? An outlaw in a filthy hovel. Diggers' dreams were useless when the woman you loved did not share them.

CHAPTER FIFTEEN

The Outlaws

Though Cutch tried to persuade me, I would not move on. I took my horse and spent long risky hours watching Markyate Manor from behind a brake of trees. On two occasions I saw carts arrive from the St Albans road; carts bearing a large polished dining table and chairs, some storage chests, and what looked like rolled tapestries. Other deliveries too, bolts of cloth, the rush-man with new rushes for the floors. In the fields around the Manor, men were hard at work, ploughing for the winter crops whilst my plot lay fallow.

When I came back after one of these journeys I was morose and bitter, and Cutch shook his head. He ignored me, but went on emptying the snares and boiling up dock and nettle to make a meal without speaking.

Finally, he spoke. 'We've been here ten days,' he said. 'I've been counting. What are we doing, Ralph?'

'What do you mean?'

'Well, we can't stay here forever. The leaves are falling and there's not as much cover.'

'Why move,' I said, 'we're safe enough here, aren't we?' And I continued to break up more kindling for our fire. Though I knew he was right, the leaf-fall was dense underfoot.

'Then I might move on without you. It would be safer for us to move independently too.'

I stopped what I was doing.

He looked serious, and guilt hit me like a ball of shot. 'You've had enough, haven't you? Can't say I blame you. I'd promised you work in the village and instead we're stuck out here. You can go on without me, if you like—'

A screaming noise made us swivel to look into the undergrowth. 'It's a deer,' Cutch said.

As we approached we could see it thrashing. One of the rabbit snares had caught round its hoof, and that in turn was caught around a thick coppiced branch that had been cut off close to the ground.

It was a doe, light-boned and graceful. At the sight of us, its eyes rolled white with fear. 'Shall I shoot it?' Cutch had his bow ready.

'No, wait,' I said. I felt sorry for it.

'You're right. It would be too much meat for just us. And it seems a shame. She's only a young one. Give us your jerkin, we'll put that over her head, quieten her.'

I unfastened my doublet, and wriggled out of the sleeves. The deer was still panicked and every movement cut deeper into its leg. I threw my doublet over its head, held it tight. Slowly the flailing legs quietened, until Cutch could get to the wire. He had to make several attempts to free the animal, and dodge its flying hooves. But finally the rabbit snare was off, and wrapped round its own peg to keep it from doing more damage.

'Here, hold her head,' Cutch said. 'I'm going to put some feverfew on that wound.'

I lay on its neck to hold it still whilst he found the herb by the edge of the track and squashed it to bring the juice. Then I tied a strip of cloth from my shirt around it, clamping the feverfew over the wound.

'Alright,' he said, 'You can let her go.'

I pulled my doublet off her head and the deer scrambled up and leapt sideways, bounding away into the forest. All we could see was the strip of white cloth on her hind leg as her natural camouflage blended her into the trees.

'You've done us out of a venison dinner,' Cutch said. 'I'm that sick of rabbit I could have eaten her raw.'

'Sorry Cutch. It just didn't seem right. You go on without me, find yourself a nice alehouse, get a decent dinner. I'm going to stay here. There's my mother and Abigail to think of. I don't trust Downall, or Thomas Fanshawe.'

'No. It's alright. I've sort of got used to you. And you couldn't manage without me, could you? Like with the deer. You need me.'

'Like a hole in the head. I'm not the one who had to mend the wagon wheel three times, and it's still not fixed. You're a crap wheelwright.' But I was smiling. I'd thought he'd leave me.

'Aye, you're probably right.' He exhaled a huge sigh. 'I'll stay on one condition,' he said. 'That I don't have to eat another rabbit.'

'Well it's that, or nettle and berries, and the berries are all but gone.'

He made a face. 'I think we can do better than that.'

'How so?'

'I've been thinking. The road. It's only a half mile off. We can relieve a few folk of their excess provisions.'

'Are you serious? I don't hold with robbery. It's against the Diggers way.'

He sighed. 'Not the flaming Diggers again. I'm sick of hearing about them. Forget them, they can't help us now, but the highway can. Think of it like robbing the rich to feed the poor.'

'Oh Cutch. I grew out of stories of Robin Hood years ago. And I'm not sure I—'

'You don't see me as Maid Marian, then?' He grinned.

'Give over!' I pushed him on the shoulder, 'I'm in enough trouble. What would happen if news got around that I'm holding up the highway?'

He shrugged. 'Might as well be hung for a sheep as for a lamb. You're an outlaw, aren't you? You'll get the blame for anything that goes on anyway.'

'But it will draw more attention to us.'

'You're on the run already, what difference will it make? It need only be once. I've done it before, it's not such a hard task. The New Model Army used to call this road the River of Gold. We relieved many a London merchant of his coin, or his provisions.'

His words took me back to a night when I met Abigail on the highway last summer, trying to hold up the Royalists on their way to the King. Silly girl. She'd got herself into a proper mess. The memory seemed so long ago. I mused over it, but Cutch was still speaking. 'Best go over Wheathamstead way, catch someone on their way back from market. Of course it'll be pot-luck what they've bought, but you can usually rely on bread and oatmeal for a start.'

The thought of proper bread made my stomach rumble. I felt myself waver.

'After that, if we have to move on again,' Cutch said, 'we'll at least be prepared, and provisioned. We can be well on our way by the time the alarm is raised.'

'No. We're not moving on. And highway robbery's a crazy idea.'

'You got a better one? Or do you want to live on rabbit stew for the rest of your life?'

CHAPTER SIXTEEN

Hold-up on the Highway

'I'm going back,' I told him. 'River of gold, you said. Well it looks like there's a drought. We've seen nobody for hours.'

Cutch was right. I'd held out a few more days, but we were constantly hungry, and rabbit stew now made me gag. For a few nights during the dark of the moon, we'd hidden in the trees by the highway, but the only folk who passed us were drovers with their flocks, and itinerant beggars with their bundles, and they looked just as ragged as ourselves, and we could not face the idea of robbing people so poor.

'Just a little longer,' Cutch said, 'we need cash too if we can get it. My blade needs sharpening and we've no whetstone. I can't make one of those out of sticks and bracken. Happen a travelling tinker will sell us one, if we can pay. And if we can get a razor we can shave, make ourselves look different.'

'What are you thinking?'

'If I looked different I could risk going to market.' Cutch fingered his pistol, which was loaded in preparation.

'Put that thing away. It makes me nervous. Better to save your powder. We could get ourselves a pheasant or two instead of—'

'Hush! Something's coming!'

I strained my ears. He was right. I dragged my scarf up over my face, tipped my hat lower. Cutch did the same, until only a white split of face remained.

Hoofbeats, and the trundle of a carriage.

'You know what you have to do,' hissed Cutch.

The white blazes of the horses were what I saw first, and the glint of silver on the coachman's livery. I gripped my reins tighter until the last moment. When the coach was almost upon us, I yelled, galloped out into their path.

The horse nearest to me stalled, the other neighed, tried to escape its traces. The carriage veered to the side, almost toppled, amid a creak of timber and metal.

'Git on!' The coachman lashed his whip, but the horses were spooked now, and trod on the spot, ears flicking back, eyes white.

I levelled my musket at the coachman's chest. 'Halt!' I cried. But he had seen the gun and was already dropping the reins.

He held up his hands. 'Don't shoot!'

A gentleman stuck his head out through the window, an older man of fifty years or more, with a grizzled moustache and white about the face. No. It couldn't be.

I fell back as if I'd been scalded. Jacob's father, Mallinson, the village constable.

'Cutch! Cutch!' I hissed, from behind my kerchief, but Cutch did not heed my frantic calls.

Of all the fingers of fate! I bent my head lower, prayed Mallinson would not recognise me, reined my horse back into the gloom of the overhanging trees.

'Drive, damn you!' Mallinson yelled at the coachman, but his servant kept his hands high.

'Get out.' Cutch leapt into view, gestured at Mallinson with his pistol.

'What the...?' Mallinson had not expected two riders. 'What the devil do you want?' he asked, jutting his chin in a display of bravado.

'What you got?' Cutch asked, his voice muffled, nosing his pistol towards him.

'Nothing. Just a sack of turnips and some eggs. From my sister's hens.'

'Hand over your purse.' Cutch said.

'I will do no such thing. I am responsible for Law and Order around here, and I'll be damned if I'll be robbed in my own village.'

'Out. Or would you rather leave your brains on the road?'

Mallinson heaved himself down, stood like an ox. Cutch pointed his pistol at Mallinson's chest. 'Stay still,' he ordered. Then he called to me, 'Search the carriage.'

I was reluctant to come into view. I saw Cutch turn to look for me, but a moment's inattention was all Mallinson needed. He bolted, dodged for the driver's seat.

'Stop him!' Cutch yelled.

A flash and a crack, and Mallinson staggered and almost fell. Cutch looked down at the gun as if he'd only just seen it.

Mallinson scrambled up next to the terrified coachman, took up the reins and yelling and cracking the whip urged the horses into a standing start. The coachman's astonished face was the last thing I saw as the carriage careered down the road.

I ripped the scarf from my face, slithered down from my horse. 'What do you think you're doing?' I shouted. 'Do you want every man jack to know we're here?'

'I didn't expect it to go off.'

'We only held up the bloody constable, didn't we?'

'What? What are you talking about?'

'That was Mallinson! Oh Lord, we're for it now. He'll have every able-bodied man on our tails quicker than lightning.'

'Why didn't you say something? Call it off?'

'I tried, but you wouldn't listen.'

Cutch shook his head in disbelief. Then he dropped down to his knees. He put his finger to the ground, brought it up to look at it. 'Blood. I must have hit him.'

'God's breath!' I tried to say more but could not even speak.

We'd shot the constable. Jacob's father. What would Abigail think? It was a disaster. I paced up and down, unable to be still. Cutch and his stupid ideas. The St Alban's road was close to our hideout, and soon people would be searching. We'd have to move on.

I mounted my horse without a word, galloped off down the track into the forest. Behind me I heard Cutch's horse crash through the undergrowth.

At the charcoal burner's cottage I dismounted and began throwing all my things into a bag.

Cutch jumped from his horse and grabbed me by the shoulder, 'Whoa! What's all this?'

I pushed him away. 'You've ruined it. We can't stay here. We'll have to move on, go places where he can't find us.'

'If he's hurt, it will be a few days before he comes looking.'

'He's Jacob's father! You shot my best friend's father! I can't believe this is happening.'

I caught the hurt in Cutch's eyes when I called Jacob my best friend.

'Sorry,' I said, 'Sorry. I didn't mean...' I held out my arms in an apology.

'Piss off,' Cutch said.

'Calm down,' I said putting a restraining arm on his shoulder. He threw up his arms to ward me off, more violently than he intended, and before I knew it my fists were up. Cutch covered his head to protect himself, an expression of disbelief on his face.

I caught myself just in time. I took a deep breath, regained some control.

Cutch exhaled. He saw my anger drain away, watched me lower my shaking hands.

'Suppose we're in deep trouble,' he said.

'You could say that.'

We packed up our bags and scattered the fire, tried to return everything to its previous condition, before setting off back through the forest taking the back roads south of the village towards Symondshyde Great Wood, the only other forest in this area that might afford us cover.

'Our horses give us away,' Cutch said. 'Best hobble them somewhere else.' He set off leading both horses with a hobbling rope slung over his shoulder.

We lived rough for three days, prayed that search parties would go North where the hold-up had happened, and not South. After that much time I was going crazy to know what was happening; if they were still looking for us. 'I'm going to go to the Manor,' I said, 'Find Abigail and talk to her, find out about Jacob's father and what's happening.'

'She'll not be pleased,' Cutch said. 'When I walked her home, she made me promise I'd get you out of the county.'

'You'd no right to promise that,' I said. 'Anyway, it's your fault we're in this mess.'

'You're on your own then. It'll be the gallows if they catch us sniffing round there.'

'Suit yourself.'

'I'm in enough trouble. Shooting a constable is a hanging offence, and I want to keep my neck, thanks very much.'

The night was bright with a three quarter moon like a broken sixpence, and I had no difficulty picking my way on foot through the trees. A bag was slung over my shoulder for any provisions I could find, and a sharp blade was sheathed in my belt. You couldn't be too careful. After the disaster with the pistol, I decided to leave firearms behind. Too risky - one wounded constable was enough.

The edge of the wood bounded the highway and then I would be on open ground. I paused to ponder my route, whether to stay close to the hedge, or whether to run for it. It was as well I did, for there were hoofbeats approaching, and the jangle of a bit.

My heart thumped in my chest. I retreated into the trees, took out my knife.

The rider was on a big dark horse, no blaze or markings. Despite the mild night, the figure wore a cloak with the collar half-up over his face and a low brimmed hat. Up to no good, was my immediate thought. I was ready to jump back in case his horse should sense me, but suddenly he pulled off the track into the wood.

Was he looking for me?

There was nowhere I could go. He'd see me if I ran for it. Panicked, I scanned my surroundings for a hiding place.

Nothing but trees. A nearby elm had a low foothold. I put my boot on it and, grabbing a branch, hauled myself silently upwards into its branches.

From this vantage point I could see the man. He was doing nothing, just sitting there, waiting. Someone else must be coming; he was waiting for someone. I dare not move.

Sure enough, a few moments later a bent old chap leading a pack-donkey approached. It was late to be out, for an old codger like him, I thought. The donkey was weighed down with a heavy wicker pannier on each side. I glanced to the horseman on my right. He was dismounting, hitching the horse to a tree.

When the cloaked stranger came into the road from the forest, the man startled, 'Ho! Made me jump,' he said crossly.

The man in the dark cloak seemed to rush towards him all at once, the cloak swirling around them both. The hiss of a sword being drawn. A small mew, like a kitten. Moments later the old chap lay on the road, unmoving. My hands began to tremble, I gripped tighter to the tree. Was he dead? I stared at the motionless heap on the road.

The donkey seemed to notice nothing amiss. It stood stoically as the man rifled through its owner's pockets, even when the highwayman extracted bundles from its panniers and threw them to the side of the road. When the thief had what he wanted, he led out his horse and loaded his saddlebags.

My hands were numb, my backside too, but I dare not shift a muscle. My stomach gave a rumble and I pressed one hand to it willing it to be silent. The man paused by his horse, looked sharply behind him.

My stomach rumbled again. The man crept over to my side of the road, peered into the undergrowth. I held my breath, prayed my stomach would be still. The man waited a few more minutes, listening, but then the donkey brayed and caught his attention.

He ran to his horse, mounted and cantered away down the road in the direction of the village. I listened to his hoof beats fading. His horse has lost a shoe, I thought. Then I realised this was a stupid thought.

Soon as he was out of earshot I almost fell out of the tree. I rushed over to the old man, but even from a few yards off I could see the sticky black stain spreading in the moonlight, and an oozing slit in the place where the collar should have been.

I bent over for a closer look. Poor old thing seemed even smaller and frailer than when he'd been upright. Some good wife would be waiting for him. What should I do? I couldn't tell anyone what I'd seen. I wandered over to the donkey, stroked its nose.

'Hello, fella. What's happened to your master, eh?' My voice was shriller than usual. 'What was that man after, hey boy?'

Hell's teeth, I was talking to a donkey. I wasn't thinking straight.

I felt in the panniers, found they were full of rounds of cheese. A cheese merchant. I wanted to laugh. It seemed ludicrous. At the same time as I had that thought, my mouth watered, and I realised I had to get out of there. If anyone else came, they'd think I'd done it. I remembered Cutch's words, that they'd blame everything on me. I gave an inward groan. Resisted the thought of that delicious cheese.

CHAPTER SEVENTEEN

Dark Encounter

My legs felt like feathers as I skulked along the hedges with the dim lights of the Manor drawing me forward through the dark. Leaving the old man in the road felt wrong. I sent prayers heavenwards for his soul. The irony of the situation had not escaped me though - how close I was to being that masked highwayman, slitting someone's throat for a few provisions. Hadn't we almost done the same? The only difference was, we hadn't deliberately set out to kill anyone. Not that anyone would believe us, of course.

There had been something ruthless and efficient in the way that masked rider had delivered the old man's death.

I turned to look over my shoulder. He'd put the fear of God into me all right.

When I got nearer to the house I stopped just outside the barn. The sweet, musty-hay smell of it almost made me choke. It seemed years ago that we had held our first Diggers meetings there; that I had looked over at Kate, her face all shiny-eyed as she listened to me lay out our Diggers plans for a free future. Her face was the only one I saw in that gathering. It had a glow about it. I remember thinking, by all that's holy, I've fallen in love.

I was getting maudlin. I pushed her from my mind. Dare not think of her somewhere inside the house - probably dining off silver platters with Thomas Fanshawe who had run away from the war and had probably never seen a dead body in his life. I forced myself to move onwards in the shadow on the outbuildings towards the yard. I scanned the shadows but could see no movement.

There was a candle still burning in the kitchen. I crept towards it. Fingers crossed it was Abigail, still up. I peered through the greenish glass.

Abigail was there, polishing the copper bottom of a cooking pot. Her back was to me, and she was rubbing slowly. I saw her shoulders rise and fall in a sigh. I went to the kitchen door but it was locked. Back to the window.

I tapped on the glass, but of course she could not hear me and I daren't tap any louder.

'Turn round,' I willed her, but she carried on rubbing at the pan.

At one point she glanced over her shoulder at the window, and I caught the glint of tears on her cheeks, saw her face was shadowed with pain. I tapped again, louder, but she did not see me out there in the dark, and turned back, stared down at the pan in her lap. In desperation I pulled out a white kerchief, flapped frantically at the window.

'Ralph!' The voice behind me made my heart seem to shoot into my mouth. I whipped round, to see Kate's wide eyes less than a foot from mine.

She grasped me by the arm, 'Quick, into the buttery. Downall's out here somewhere.'

I followed her into the cool, windowless darkness, heard the rustle of her skirts on the flagstone floor, the soft thud as she closed the heavy wooden door behind us. 'What are you doing here?' she whispered. 'Don't you know half the county's searching for you?'

'I came to see Abigail.'

A pause. 'Not me?' Her joking voice held a trace of disappointment.

'I hear your husband is back. Abigail told me of your plans for the house. They didn't include me.' My whisper echoed strangely in the dark, but I could not keep the jealous tone out of it.

'Fool. I care nothing for Thomas,' she said. 'My heart is taken already, by a blond gentleman farmer who wants to change the world.' Her words hung in the blackness.

A sudden miaow.

Kate muffled her cry of surprise as soon as it escaped her lips. We both bent over to find the cause of the noise.

'It's only the cat,' she whispered, 'he must have followed us in.' I stretched out my hand to feel for it, and my fingers found the back of her hand as she stroked the cat's soft fur. I closed my hand over hers, caressed her thumb with a gentle touch.

Time stretched, I could hear her breathing. The feeling of her soft skin made me want to cry. Suddenly I was overwhelmed. I pulled her to upright, felt for her face with my fingers, but only found the starched linen of her collar. I traced my way up to her chin, and onto her lips. Her mouth opened to let my fingers in. So soft, so tender. The sharpness of her little teeth opening to her tongue.

Urgently I put my mouth there, kissing her long and deep, drinking in her woman's smell of starch and roses.

Outside, the noise of boots on the cobbles.

I froze like a tree to the spot, dare not even breathe.

The cat miaowed again, I felt it twine around my legs, pressing for attention.

The noise of a flint striking steel, and then the pungent smell of pipe smoke. I squeezed Kate's hand. A familiar cough from just outside the door.

God's breath, Downall. And he was less than two yards away. I felt Kate dip down to quieten the cat, but I guess she could not find it, because the next thing we knew there was an almighty crash, the sound of rolling wood and metal. A pail falling off the shelf. I dragged Kate behind the door just in time as it swung open, nearly flattening us to the wall.

All I could see was a bulk blocking the doorway with a red glow of a pipe in the middle of it.

The cat shot past Downall with a screech.

'Bastard cat,' he said. Then he pulled the door shut with a slam.

He hadn't seen us. I sagged with relief. My heart was pounding like a hammer on an anvil. The wooden pail rolled back and forth, the iron bands making a metallic rhythm of their own.

The pail creaked to a standstill and the footsteps receded across the yard. Kate's hand still gripped mine so tight her nails dug in my palm. When we were sure he'd gone, she said, 'He doesn't seem to sleep. He...' I heard her sigh, search for words.

'What?'

'He bullies Thomas. He knows that Thomas was for the King and he threatens him —says he's watching him, and he'll report him if he contacts any other known Royalist sympathisers.'

'Thomas is his employer for God's sake! Why doesn't he just sack him?'

'Because Thomas made a pact with Mallinson. And to be honest, I think Mallinson's afraid of Downall too. And there's more. A highway thief shot at Mallinson on the London road, and Downall has convinced him it was you. Of course I tried to persuade them they were wrong, but Jacob's broken it off with Abigail because of it.'

I shuffled uncomfortably. 'The bastard. It's not her fault.'

Now I knew why Abigail had been crying. The needle of guilt had become sharper now.

Kate touched my arm gently. 'I must go, Ralph. They'll be looking for me in the house. I only came out because I wanted to check the number of chickens in the hen huts. Abigail is convinced a few more disappear each day, and not to the fox, but to Downall's table. Shall I tell her to come out to you?'

I changed my mind. I could not bear to see Abigail; not now. I felt too guilty. And besides, Kate had told me what I needed to know.

'Shall I fetch her?' Kate asked again.

'No. It was you I wanted to see. And I'll only add to her troubles if Downall catches us. Tell her not to worry. I'll go and talk to Jacob, make it right with him somehow. Tell her to let Mother know how I am.'

I embraced her, and she clung tight to me, her head resting on my chest. When she withdrew, the unspoken question of when I might see her again hung on my lips. She read it in my face but stopped it my bringing her lips to mine.

Suddenly I was lost. I kissed her neck, her arms, any inch of bare skin I could find, nudging down the chemise where it curved over the swell of her breasts to kiss her there too. She kissed me back, urgently, brought her hand down the front of my shirt. We shouldn't be doing this, every part of me knew it to be wrong, and dangerous and begging for trouble. But her hands roamed over my chest and the sensation made me shiver and tremble with longing.

Within moments we were on the flagstone floor, our limbs tangled together. When I fumbled for the cords of my breeches, she rolled up her skirts. Her pale thighs gleamed in the moonlight, they opened to welcome me in.

When we had done, we held each other close. 'My Kate,' I murmured, drunk on her touch.

In the distance a door slammed.

Kate sat up, pulled down her skirts, 'Downall. The stable door. He sleeps there now.'

'Are you alright?' I asked.

'Don't come here again,' she said, her voice husky with emotion, 'not until they catch the man who shot Mallinson. Folks are already saying...'

'I know, I know.' They would be saying it was me.

A flash of the image of the old man, up on the road, his breath stopped. Should I say anything? I bit my tongue. Life was complicated enough. Barely had I had time to think this, when I realised Kate was gone. The door was swinging, a pale stripe of moonlight widening and narrowing over my feet.

CHAPTER EIGHTEEN

Three Crows

'You can't be serious?' Cutch put down the flagon he was drinking from. 'It'll be walking into the lion's mouth!'

'I need to talk to Jacob, tell him to make it up with Abigail.'

'You realise you're risking my neck too? Will you tell him it was me who shot at his father?'

'No. I'll tell him it was me, but that I'll keep away from here from now on. That they need not see me again.' I had not told Cutch I'd seen Kate. The memory was too precious to speak of. But I had resolved to go away. However much it pained me, it seemed the best I could do for Abigail and the family. And now I feared that the temptation to see Kate would be even stronger.

Cutch whistled softly. 'You can't do that. Will you really go?'

I nodded. It would do Kate no good to be associated with a known felon, and I could not risk someone finding us together.

'You've changed your tune,' Cutch said. 'I'm coming with you to Jacob's then. I don't trust you not to blurt it all out, tell him it was me.'

'Oh, thanks for your confidence. I won't sneak on you. But I was thinking about that highway robbery I told you about. Abigail was right; as long as I'm anywhere near here, I'll get blamed for every hold-up on that road. I want to tell Jacob what I saw. That highwayman shouldn't get away with it. The victim was only an old man, doing nobody any harm. And I want to make it right between Jacob and Abigail before I go — want to know she's being looked after, that someone will keep an eye on Mother when I'm gone.'

'What about—?'

'Don't.' I snapped, held my hand up to ward off more questions.

'That bad is it? Remind me never to get involved with a woman. Cause no end of trouble.'

Jacob's cottage was on the edge of the village on the far side of the village green. We went early, before first light. The only person we passed was a milkmaid slouching along, her yoke heavy with milk. When we saw her coming we took our horses into the shadow of the church. After she'd gone, we tied them in Jacob's orchard, and went in the back way, past the neatly kept vegetable plot. The sight of it made me angry, when mine was lying fallow.

I rapped at the door. Nobody answered so I tried the latch and found it open.

We were barely over the threshold when a white shape leapt from the sleeping loft, wild eyed, dressed only in a nightshirt and breeches. Within an instant, a short sword was wrapped round my neck.

'S'truth, Ralph!' Jacob released me and pushed me away. 'I thought you were—'

'Sorry to wake you so early,' I said, relieved to still have my head intact.

'What in hellfire do you think you're doing?' Jacob's face was beet red, his hair loose and wild.

'We've come to talk to you,' I said.

I deliberately put off my sword, and Cutch laid his beside it.

Jacob looked us over, but kept his sword out in front of him. 'I was asleep! What time do—'

'Don't make a fuss, I just need to talk, that's all. And we haven't eaten for days. A bit of breakfast wouldn't go amiss.' I smiled, watched his expression become less guarded.

'You can't stay. My father's got men stripping the woods looking for you.'

'I know. People keep telling me that. I've been to the Manor.'

'Oh.' Jacob had the grace to look guilty.

'It's not her fault, Jacob. Not Abigail's fault she's got a rotten brother that keeps getting himself into trouble. Come on, let's sit. I only want a few moments of your time.' I pulled out a chair and sat down. Cutch stayed standing, I guess he didn't trust my mouth.

'He shot my father.' Jacob pointed to Cutch. So they'd worked it out. 'They recognised your horses.'

'It was an accident,' Cutch said. 'I was aiming for the horse's leg, but your father got in the way somehow.'

'You expect me to believe that? It's a long way from a horse's fetlock to a shoulder.'

'It's the truth,' I said. 'He's a bad shot.'

Cutch was about to protest but thought better of it. 'Sorry. It was a pig's ear of a shot. How is he, your father?'

'How do you think? He's got a shot-hole in his shoulder the size of a plum. You were holding up his carriage, for God's sake!'

'So would you,' I said, 'if you'd got nothing to eat and no other way of survival. We didn't know it was your father, and we didn't mean—'

'Get out.' Jacob's voice held a warning. He threw his sword down on the table in front of me. 'I can't have you here. What happened to all your ideals of non-violence, Ralph? You're not the man I knew. I don't want you in my house.'

The old Ralph would have fought back, but I was worn out with war. The war outside me, and the war inside me. I'd done nothing but fight since I was two years old.

First my father, then the aristocracy, now my family and friends.

I picked up Jacob's sword and lay it down at my feet. 'I'm the same man, Jake. Same person who used to watch out for someone coming while you scrumped for apples. No, I tell a lie. I'm not the same man. Nobody could watch grown Englishmen tear each other's throats out, and stay the same.' I tried and failed, to keep the quaver from my voice. I looked up at his frowning expression, shrugged. 'I'll go then. I can see I have no friend here.'

Jacob's expression shifted, softened. He shook his head. 'You're a fool, Ralph Chaplin. Your own worst enemy. A few minutes then.' He glanced towards Cutch. 'But he can wait outside, keep watch in case someone comes.' Cutch raised his eyebrows at me.

'Would you mind?' I asked.

'Guess someone had better do it,' Cutch grumbled. He grabbed his sword and sheathing it, headed for the door. I watched his short squat figure go. A hat was lying on the side table. It looked familiar. I stared at its green velvet ribbon, its trimming of green and scarlet feathers. Scarlet - a mite ostentatious for an apothecary's girl, I had thought.

'That's Elizabeth's hat,' I pointed. 'What's it doing here?'

'Oh. She must have left it behind.'

'But why?' I was immediately suspicious. 'What was she doing here?'

'She came to ask after you.'

'A likely story.' Any excuse to get her conniving smile over his threshold.

'No, someone came to the apothecary's looking for you. She thought I might know him, an old friend of yours.'

'Who? One of Downall's men no doubt, after my hide.'

'Not that I know of. A stranger.'

'What did he look like?'

Elizabeth said he was 'an arrogant dog who thought he was better than her.' She didn't tell him anything. She pretended not to know you. But he must be pretty keen to find you, because he'd asked at the blacksmith's too. He told him you'd...how shall

I say? Moved on. Said if anyone knew where you'd gone it would likely be your mother.'

'How do you know all this?'

'I called in to the smith's to get some nails. My thatch needs fixing. The man had been there just before me to get his horse shod. A big black beast by all accounts.'

I was silent. There was only one horse I knew that matched that description. The one I'd seen last night. The murdering bastard who'd killed that old man.

But why was he looking for me? I was about to tell Jacob about him, but then I thought better of it. If they thought he was a friend of mine, it might get me into more trouble.

'Look, Elizabeth only came to see if I knew where you were, and I didn't, so she went away.'

I'll bet, I thought. And I bet she was wearing her best Sunday frock and a simpering smile to match.

'I'm sorry about Abigail,' Jacob said. 'It's a mess. I never meant to hurt her. It's just...my father won't have it, and it's not fair to keep her dangling.'

'Don't you care about her?'

'What do you think? Of course I do. I can't stop thinking about her. It's worse now. I keep seeing her face when I told her it was over. She looked...resigned. It made me feel such a toad.'

'Then talk to your father again. I'm going away. I won't come back, not for years. You can all stop looking for me, because I'll be gone.'

He looked crestfallen, now the reality of my leaving hung between us. 'Where will you go?'

'Don't know. London maybe. Join a ship. Get as far away from Markyate Manor as possible.'

'What about Kate?'

'Will you stop asking me about Kate! What is it with everyone? She's married isn't she! To bloody Thomas Fanshawe.' Jacob held up his hands in surrender. 'And that's another thing,' I said. 'Downall's bullying the Fanshawes, I don't like the sound of it. He's up to something.'

'What do you expect me to do about it? I'm not Downall's keeper.'

'I don't know, warn your father. Tell him he's not to be trusted. By the way, Kate thinks he's bullying him too.'

'Who? My father? Can't see anyone browbeating him.'

'I don't know; he ran pretty fast when Cutch pointed a pistol at him.'

'Hang on,' Jacob said, 'I thought you told me Cutch was aiming for the horse?'

I heard the rise in Jacob's voice, tried to placate him, 'He was, he was. Don't get riled on me again.'

'He's a flaming liability, your friend. What on earth made you take up with *him*?'

I stared. Jacob couldn't be jealous, could he?

'These mercenaries. I've seen his type. He'll have no loyalty at all, just go on the side that's paying.'

'I know he's a bit rough round the gills, but—'

A noise behind me alerted me to Cutch's figure just disappearing from out of the doorway. He must have heard us.

'Cutch!'

But by the time I got outside he'd leapt onto his horse. His mouth was set in a grim line, and he kicked his horse into a gallop straight at me. 'What the—!' I hurled myself sideways, into the hedge. I scrambled up, but he was off away down the lane, hooves flying. He did not look back. Jacob appeared beside me.

'Oh Lord,' I said. 'He heard us. I'll have to go after him.'

'Let him go. Look to yourself,' Jacob said. 'There's still men searching for you out there.'

But there was an unease in my belly. Cutch had done nothing but support me all these weeks and now it felt like I'd pissed on him.

'Sorry Jacob, but he's my friend.'

Still keeping to untrodden byways and the little known tracks through the forest, I returned to where

Cutch and I had spent the previous night. Our branch and bracken shelter was empty. Wind had blown the remainder of the leaves from the trees, so the branches were bare. There was no sign of Cutch. Horseflies buzzed around where we'd slept, and over the rotting remains of the meat we'd kicked into the brush. I went to look at the spot where we'd tethered the horses. Nothing but dung. So he hadn't been back here.

He'd really gone. I couldn't quite believe it. Couldn't imagine what it would be like to live wild without him. What would happen if he got caught? They'd torture the truth out of him; that was the way of the Assizes. They'd have the truth they wanted, or something masquerading as it, because everyone loved a hanging.

What was it with men and death? They'd spend half their lives trying to avoid it; with physicians and herbs and God knows what all else, and then half their lives courting it; with their leaping to war or a duel on the slightest provocation.

I sat down a moment to think. That man who'd been looking for me – could he have seen me, hiding in that tree? Was that why he was looking for me, because I'd witnessed him killing that old man?

The blacksmith had sent him on to my mother's house. The hairs on my neck bristled, I could not contain a shiver. I stood and paced up and down. It was probably all right. But then again, I did not like the sound of it. Something wasn't right. Was it some sort of trap?

Would Jacob lie to me so that his father could find me? I dismissed that thought. Jacob was far too law-abiding to try any tricks.

I un-tethered the horse, slapped its neck. 'Sorry, old boy, but we've got to go back to Markyate.'

When we got nearer to the village I thought I would be less obtrusive on foot, so I left Titan tethered in the woods. To be safe, I had armed myself with my pistol and powder, and with my backsword and the trusty knife. As I came to the edge of the woods, my eye was caught by a flapping white paper pinned to a large oak.

WANTED
Ralph Chaplin, Highwayman.
For the murders of
John Silverskin, Cheesemaker,
William Gawston, Tinker,
and the attempted murder of
Constable John Mallinson.
For the speedy apprehending of this malicious
Traitor to the Peace of this Commonwealth,

> *Parliament doth straitly charge and*
> *command all Officers, Civil and Military,*
> *and all other good People of this Nation,*
> *That they make diligent enquiry for the said*
> *Felon and his Abettors, and Adherents,*
> *And, being apprehended, to bring before the*
> *Parliament, or Council of State,*
> *to be proceeded with as Justice shall require.*

More of Mallinson's ridiculous wordiness followed, but I'd seen enough. But who was this other man, Gawston? If the highway thief had killed someone else as well...I speeded my step.

In the back of my mind the thought of Edward Copthorne ran round like a rat in a trap. It could have been him on the road, but then again, I couldn't be sure. He was tall enough to be the highway thief, but I couldn't tell with that standing collar covering half his face. I wished I could be certain. I'd forgotten him, but now someone was looking for me... a trickle ran down my spine, as if I'd been drenched with cold water.

I paused behind the wall before I could cross the field to mother's back garden. Goodwife Boardman was outside her cottage next door, hanging up her washing over a line, and I did not want her to see me go in. Strange – Mother's shutters were closed. It was unusual at this time of the day. But then again, it was going to be another scorcher of a day, so maybe Mother had decided to keep them closed. My attempt to reassure myself with reason did not work.

A harsh cawing. I looked up. Three black crows had landed on the roof, were pecking at the thatch. My heart started to ache in a way that I did not like.

Goodwife Boardman went back inside and I slipped like a stoat past her washing. The door was ajar. I pushed it open.

'Mother?'

No answer. I squinted, let my eyes get used to the gloom. It was eerily silent. Usually at this time my little sister Martha would be at the table with her handloom.

'Mother?'

I could not move any further into the room. There was something by the hearth. Mother's iron-soled clog. It stopped me in my tracks. I'd never seen the underside of her shoes before. Behind the chair, one bare foot in a pale stocking. On the cold flag floor. She was twisted at an awkward angle, the linen of her summer petticoat showing white under her cotton skirts. No. She wouldn't like showing her shift. But even from here I knew that her head was not hanging how it should. Blood. Too much blood. Dizzy. Get me out. Out.

I staggered to the front door, clung to the doorframe, hung over. Not sick. Not now. It was not real. I'd go back in, in a minute, and she'd call out, 'Ah, t'is you!' just the way she always had. There was something else, something nagging at the corner of his mind. A surge of hot fear took my knees from under me. I gripped the doorpost more tightly before turning and going back inside.

'Martha?' I called.

No reply.

William? Where was William? One glance in the crib was enough. His face was just the same as when he was sleeping. Smooth, unlined, innocent. His little lips slightly open beneath a button nose. I almost expected him to cry. Except that he couldn't. Not with that kitchen knife still in his chest like that.

'Martha!' I shouted, ran up the rickety stairs to the sleeping loft, threw aside pillows and bedding. Back down, out the back door. Into the stall where the cow chewed and looked at me with doleful eyes. No Martha. I leapt into the yard, yelling her name, not caring that Goodwife Boardman would hear. The chickens ignored my frenzied shouts, scratched their elegant talons in the dust.

Then I heard it, a noise, from the hen hutch, the sound of singing. 'Lavender's blue, dilly dilly...'

I flung the door open.

'Ralfie!' She was crouching there, lining up the eggs in a row, instead of putting them in her basket. She smiled at me, grabbed hold of the knee of my breeches, her curly hair full of wisps of straw. 'Help me count the eggs?'

I dropped to my knees, enfolded her to my chest, hugged her tight. Thank God, thank God.

'Ouch!' She wriggled down. 'Hurts. How many?'

'Five. Yes, five.' It surprised me I could still count.

'Let's show Mother.'

I grabbed her by the hand. My mind raced, sorting through all the possibilities. 'No. Mother's poorly, she needs some quiet time. We'll go to the church, to the Vicarage?'

'Shall I bring the eggs?'

'Yes, yes. Bring them. But be quick.'

'Carry!'

Usually I would make her walk, but not today. I scooped her up, ran to the Vicarage, hammered on the door. When it opened, Goodwife Preston tried to close the door, but I forced it open, pushed Martha through.

'Don't be afraid,' I said desperately, knowing my reputation as a ruffian. 'Please. I need you to keep Martha safe. Don't let her go outside, don't let any strangers in. Promise?' Goodwife Preston took a hard look at my face, and shepherded Martha inside, 'Eggs! How lovely. Go on in, dear, and put them on the table.'

Once Martha was out of earshot she asked, 'What is it? What ails you?'

'Someone has...' I swallowed, 'My mother is dead. And my brother. Murdered, both. Send your husband to her house to pray for their souls. I can't stay. You know why.'

'You must come in. I know my husband would want to—'

'No. They'll arrest me if they find me. Please, just keep Martha safe until Abigail can come for her.'

I blundered away from there with my world all in pieces. The fact Martha had survived had blunted the reality of the scene in my mother's cottage. Now it came back in grisly detail. Somehow I blundered my way to the woods, struggled onto Titan. A few moments later and I trotted up the main highway, dazed.

It was odd to trot, just like I was going to market on any ordinary day. A cottager who was drawing water from the pump on the green, stopped and pointed me out to his neighbour. Only then did I realise what he was doing, and that I shouldn't be on the open road. At the next bridleway I turned into the shade of the woods. Birds were singing, the field poppies still flowering. It didn't make sense. Blood seemed to hang in my nostrils.

I needed to think. What should I do? They'd have to be buried. What if it really was Copthorne who'd done this? I should tell someone. But who? Not the Constable.

Best not to think. It couldn't be Copthorne. Couldn't have anything to do with him. Just ride. Ride back. Find Cutch. He'd know what to do. Where was Cutch when I needed him?

CHAPTER NINETEEN

A Plan

My body moved, though my mind was numb. I tethered Titan on a loose rein so he could graze. A while later, I heard hoofbeats but I did not move. Nothing seemed to matter.

I stared at the grass as if it was strange stuff, the like of which I'd never seen before. Soft stuff, like a woman's hair. Yet my horse was eating it. Why?

Nothing made sense. I was orphaned, the sharp sense of being parentless in the world, was a physical pain. Father and Mother both dead. And little William.

I made an effort to think. I seemed to have lost myself, lost who I was.

The horse's chest crashed through the undergrowth and its hooves cut into the turf as it skidded to a stop.

Cutch leapt off, 'Downall's planning a rebellion,' he said breathlessly. 'I overheard him at the 'Star and Ship' and Copthorne—' Cutch crouched down beside me. 'What's happened?'

'My mother and my brother. Both dead.' When I said the words it felt like I was lying, that it couldn't be true.

'Who? Tell me.'

I told Cutch everything I could remember.

'Listen,' Cutch said, 'It's Copthorne. He's here, in Markyate. I was coming to tell you.'

My insides dropped. 'How can you be sure?'

'The cellarman at the Star and Ship. Said a stranger had just been in, asking after directions to the Manor. I paid up quick, and followed the man at a little distance. I'm sure it's Copthorne, I caught a glimpse of his face. Same pointy snout and arrogant sneer. He turned to look when he heard my horse, but I kept my head down, looked as if I was ambling home drunk. Sure enough, he turned down the drive to the Manor on his big black beast.'

I was already on my feet, so light-headed I was almost staggering. 'The Manor? I've got to go there. He'll be after Abigail.'

'I'll come with you,' Cutch gave me his cupped hands to leg me up into the saddle. 'Look Ralph, go slow. Don't rush in, it might make things worse—'

'What could be worse?' I was already setting off at a canter. I turned to yell over my shoulder. 'We need to get her out of there. Her and Kate.'

'Abigail won't realise, will she?' Cutch shouted, already kicking his horse on after me. I reined my horse to a stop to wait for him. 'She won't know about...' Cutch paused, looked away. He could not speak of my mother and William. 'Listen Ralph, we need to get in quietly. If Copthorne sees us coming, he might do something rash. We shouldn't risk it. Please, just think a moment.'

'No time.' I slapped my heels again into Titan's flank and set off along the track, ducking my head under the whipping branches. I heard Cutch's horse panting to keep up. By the time we got to the road I'd re-considered, and could see that Cutch had a point.

'You're right,' I said. 'Their best chance will be to sneak in, and then get them out quietly.'

'There's another problem,' Cutch shouted. 'Downall. He's rallying some men to throw the Fanshawes off their lands. He had some sort of disagreement with Thomas Fanshawe over the stealing of grain and livestock. Thomas had reported him to Mallinson.'

I reined to a halt. 'How do you know? Have you seen Kate?'

'No. I was mad as hell. I'd had it with you and that snooty Jacob, so I went to the tavern. I was going to turn you in, tell them where to find you.'

'Did you?'

'Would have. But thought I'd have a few first, take the edge of it all. But then Downall and his cronies arrived. I kept my head down and listened. Sounds as if Thomas turfed him out for stealing. Made Downall furious. He was raging against the Fanshawes like a bull. Now he's set on taking the estate for Parliament.'

'Mallinson won't have it, surely?'

'I'm not so sure, half the village is on Downall's side by the looks of it. John Soper's stirred them up, saying you and Kate Fanshawe broke his son's arm. Wouldn't like to be in your Kate's shoes when they arrive. He's mustering a small army.'

'Oh God. When?'

'Tonight.'

'Then we must hurry.'

I could die, I knew that. From what Cutch had told me about my father, Copthorne deserved his revenge, and I'd seen him not only fight in battle, but kill in cold blood. But if I'd been at home like I should have been, instead of on the run, Mother and William might still be alive. Guilt made me want to curl up by the hedge and never come out.

I swallowed. I'd have to face him, even though my insides were churning like a whirlpool.

'Best lead the horses to the old barn, then go on foot,' I managed. 'I went that way a few days ago.'

'Did you see Abigail?'

'No, but...'

'Don't tell me. You went to see *her*.'

I did not answer.

'Fool,' Cutch said. 'You always have to stick your neck out, don't you?'

We tethered our mounts behind the barn. 'You stay here a moment. I'll go and check if Copthorne's horse is still in the stables,' Cutch said, 'then have a squint at what's going on in the house. At least if they catch me, I can make some excuse.'

Cutch gave me the thumbs up from the stables. So Copthorne's horse was there. Cutch scuttled across the yard, half-crouched, and crept round the side of the house, looking for the windows.

Thank God dusk was falling and he would be less easily seen.

It was an agony of waiting. I chewed at the quicks of my nails, until he came running back to me.

'He's in there,' he said breathlessly. 'He's in the parlour, sitting right next to Kate. There's a fire lit, and he's talking to Thomas Fanshawe. They look friendly, like they know each other.'

'What about Abigail?'

'I saw her in the back dining room, putting glasses and sherry sack on a tray.'

I exhaled a sigh of relief. 'Thank God.'

'The back door's locked. When I peered through the window, Abigail looked up and I knocked to get her attention, but she couldn't have seen me out here in the dark, because she turned and took the tray through to the parlour.'

'She wouldn't have heard you. She's deaf, remember? We've got to get inside.'

'How?'

'The front door's too close to the parlour windows. I guess all we can do is get in the back somehow, try to overwhelm him. I'll go for Copthorne, and you must try to get Kate and Abigail clear.'

'What about Thomas Fanshawe?'

'I don't know. He's the wild card. I've no idea whether he'll fight or run. But we've got surprise on our side. Try to get the girls to the horses. Tell Abigail... not to go home. Send them to Jacob's.'

We checked our swords, I primed my pistol.

'Cutch,' I reached out to touch him on the shoulder. 'Thanks. You've been a good friend. The best.'

'Stop that nonsense. I'm a rough old dog, and I know it. No heroics though. In and out. We don't want to get mixed up with Downall and his men.'

CHAPTER TWENTY

Cavaliers and Rebels

The window to the pantry was open just a crack. I prised it open as wide as it would go. 'Look,' I whispered to Cutch, 'can you squeeze through that?'

'What do you think I am? A blooming ferret?'

'Sssh. You'll have to take your tackle off,' I said.

Cutch unbuckled his sword and I gave him a leg up. He slithered rather elegantly through, and a moment after the door to the kitchen opened. Cutch grinned, offered a mock bow. I frowned and thrust his sword back at him, just as a ginger streak shot between my legs into the house.

'Flaming cat,' Cutch said.

We tiptoed inside, Cutch with his hand on his scabbard to stop it rattling. Gently, I unsheathed my pistol and crept down the hallway, avoiding the rushes strewn near the door, in case their rustling should give us away. Outside the parlour door I paused, straining to hear.

A soft, high-pitched voice. An aristocratic voice that could not help but irritate me— Thomas, talking of his grandiose plans for the estate. 'We'll re-build the stable block with four new stalls and a bigger hay-loft above. Might build a new coach house too.'

'Sounds like a good idea. How many carriages do you keep?' Copthorne's voice was pleasantly oily. Bastard.

A loud miaow by my boot made me jerk and almost pull my trigger. I froze. I tried to move the cat with my boot, and Cutch tried to pick it up and move it away, but it yowled indignantly and carried on nosing at the door. Plaintive miaows filled the hall. Stupid animal.

'What's that?' Copthorne's voice.

'Just the cat. I thought she was outside. I'll go and let her in,' Kate said.

Cutch and I exchanged glances. As soon as she opened the door they'd see us. It had to be now.

I turned the handle and pushed the door open hard. Kate was just on the other side of it. She shot backwards into the room. Then everything happened at once. Cutch made an attempt to grab Kate by the arm, but she was confused and thrust him away. 'What the..? Leave go!'

'Ralph?' Abigail dropped the tray of glasses on the side table, where they shivered and chinked.

'Get up,' I said, pointing my pistol at Copthorne.

In one glance I took in the pair of pistols at his belt, and no sword. Copthorne did not budge, but Thomas stood slowly. He was smaller than I thought, head and shoulders below me, but his navy velvet coat was immaculately tailored, his brown hair neatly oiled to his head. He spoke in a sing-song as if talking to an idiot. 'Now put that gun down, Chaplin.'

I swung my pistol to face him, and he backed off hurriedly, hands up.

Cutch had Copthorne covered with his pistol and at the same time was trying to shepherd Kate out.

She threw off his guiding hand. 'What is all this?'

'Abigail, Kate,' I said, in my firmest most measured tone, 'Go outside and wait there.' Neither of them showed the slightest sign of doing what I asked.

'What do you want, Ralph? Haven't you caused enough trouble?' Abigail shook her head in disbelief.

I kept my pistol trained on Copthorne's chest. 'Outside. Now. We won't do this in sight of the ladies.'

'I don't understand,' Kate said. 'Mr Copthorne is our guest—'

'Whatever cock and bull tale he's told you, this man is not to be trusted,' I said without turning my head. I wasn't going to risk taking my eyes off him.

Copthorne patted the arm of the chair, one leg crossed nonchalantly over the other. 'A challenge, huh? I won't lower myself to duel with the likes of you. Shoot if you must,' he said carelessly, 'you should be wiping my boots, like the rest of your class, isn't that so, Fanshawe?'

Thomas's expression was troubled. He did not know how to reply. His mouth opened, then closed again.

Cutch glanced over, waiting for me to act, but I was at a loss. I'd expected Copthorne to fight, to draw his sword. I could not shoot him in cold blood, sitting in a chair, and he knew it. He was watching me through narrowed eyes.

'You've had your revenge Copthorne,' I tried. 'There's been enough bloodshed. Lord knows I'm sorry for what my father did, but you've had your revenge. Cromwell's defeated you. The war's done, we should let it go, get back to our lives.'

'Not whilst there's a King should be on his throne, and the devil lives on in Cromwell's army. Fanshawe agrees with me, don't you?'

Thomas dismissed him with a shake of his head. He turned to me, 'Whatever it is you want, it's best solved through talking like sensible men, not coming in here frightening my wife half to death.'

'My wife.' The words rang in my ears.

I jerked my pistol towards Copthorne. My vow to be reasonable evaporated. A red haze had sprung up in front of my eyes. I pictured my mother and William, lying where I'd left them, on the cold floor. 'You murdering bastard,' I could barely get the words out. 'Get up.'

'Abigail, talk to your brother,' Thomas appealed, 'make him see sense.'

'Ralph, please—' Abigail began to speak but I cut her off.

'No,' I shouted at her. 'You don't understand.'

Copthorne's hand moved towards his belt. I caught his movement and took a step closer. 'Don't try it,' I said, 'or I'll blow you to Kingdom Come.'

I had to get him out of there. I took a step nearer, but without warning he catapulted up out of his chair.

Abi gasped, took an involuntary step back, but she was too late. Copthorne snaked a hand round her shoulder, to try to take hold of her neck. Taken by surprise, she staggered backwards, landed heavily against the side table. It toppled and the tray and glasses fell to the floor in a shatter of glass. Copthorne seized Abigail's arm and wrenched it up behind her, forcing her up onto tiptoes. She gave a yelp of pain, 'Ralph?'

My pistol was useless in my hand. Too late to fire. I might miss, catch Abigail instead.

'What was it your father did?' Copthorne said. 'Oh yes, he took my family outside, lined them up against the wall. Want to know what that feels like? To watch your little brother weep in terror?' In one smooth movement Copthorne released Abi's arm, pulled out his pistol and pressed it to her neck.

Abigail could not have heard him, but she'd felt the gun against her skin and caught his intention. She'd been struggling, twisting like an eel, but now she was still, terrified to move. Copthorne dragged her backwards with startling efficiency. He took the gun away from her neck to loose one shot over her shoulder at me, but Abigail jerked to try to free herself. Above me, the ceiling splintered, and a shower of plaster dust peppered my shoulders.

Copthorne backed away down the hall half-throttling Abigail with an arm clamped around the neck. She was still, like a doll, one lace trailing from her boot.

Careful. I steadied my aim. *Easy now, watch out for Abigail.* My finger hovered on the trigger. Damn. I couldn't get a clear view. It was then I heard the noise outside. Like a rumble. And voices. Where were they coming from?

The distraction was enough for Copthorne to drag open the front door and push Abigail outside, hustle her back against the wall. I flew after them just in time to see him prepare to press the pistol to her temple.

It was now or never.

I fired. Sparks flew from my pan, the backfire jerked the pistol up. Copthorne's pistol discharged fractionally after mine, but thank heaven my shot had hit him and he misfired. The ball whistled up into the air. Abigail sank to her knees, whimpering prayers, covering her head.

The smell of singed cloth filled my nostrils. I saw Copthorne clutch his upper arm, where my bullet had grazed him.

A short wiry figure shot out from the shadows behind me and dragged Abigail to her feet and round the side, round the wall of the buttery. Cutch. Thank God.

The wall next to my ear spattered me with brick. Copthorne was still firing at me. Instinctively I ducked, shoved my pistol back in my belt and unsheathed my sword before he had time to reload. I was halfway across the yard when I glanced to the left. The drive was a mass of wavering torches.

A chant reached my ears, '*Beat the devils out! Beat the devils out!*'

Copthorne turned to look but suddenly the yard was full of people. With dread I saw the silhouettes of spades and forks and cudgels.

'There's one!' came a shout.

Copthorne took one look at them and sprinted for the house. One of the men raised his shovel and brought it down hard. I winced as it glanced off Copthorne's shoulder, but he did not seem to feel it, he kept on running, clutching his upper arm.

Kate and Thomas were standing in the open doorway of the Manor, but they saw Copthorne coming and heaved the door shut. Not quite in time. Copthorne hurled his weight at it and the door gave. Moments later he was behind it. I heard the rasp of metal as the bolts slid home.

Shit. I had to get out of there before the mob saw me.

I flung open the door of the buttery, and dived inside. To my surprise, Cutch and Abigail were there, pressed against the wall. Abigail's eyes were pools of fear. I grabbed her hand, squeezed it tight.

'What the hell's going on?' Cutch hissed.

'Put your back to the door! Downall's rebels. They're in the yard.'

I peered out through the stone slot window. In the dark people milled round the back of the house. There must have been hundreds of them. I smelt ale and sweat. They hammered and shoved at the door, rained a few blows. I pressed my back to the door alongside Cutch.

The door shook with a thump that sent vibrations ricocheting up my spine. But when the door did not give, they gave up. It was obvious the main body of men were at the front of the house. The chant, 'Devils out, devils out,' came from the front lawns.

I risked taking a peek through the window. Like bees on the swarm the yard suddenly emptied.

'They've gone round the front,' I said.

The chanting suddenly stopped. 'What now?' I whispered.

'Come out, by order of Parliament!' came a loud voice.

'Downall,' I said.

'Thomas Fanshawe! Don't make me break down your door. This house it to be given up by order of the Protector. No harm will come to you if you come out quietly.'

I took Cutch to one side, turned my face away so Abigail could not read me. 'Take care of Abigail. Make your way to Jacob's soon as you can get away. I'm going into the house.'

'Don't be crazy. Downall and his rabble will soon be all over, and he'll relish the chance to get even—'

'I've got to. Copthorne's in there with them. He's unhinged. You know what he did to my family. And I fear for Kate. Thomas is useless, they won't be able to hold them off on their own.'

'And you think you can?' He shook his head. 'Wait a minute. Whose side are you on, Ralph?' Cutch grabbed me by the shoulders. 'Think! You might not like Downall, but these men are doing what we fought for. Taking back our lands from those who have controlled it too long. What will you do? Fight with Fanshawe and Copthorne on the Royalist side?"

I hadn't seen it like that. It stunned me.

'Well?'

'I don't know.' I twisted away from him. 'I'm sick of 'sides.' Kate's in there. I've got to get her out. Copthorne'd slit her throat without thinking twice. And there's a rampaging mob at her door.'

'You know they'll kill you. You'll be giving them a cast iron excuse to—'

'Ralph? What is it?' Abigail appeared between us. In the dark she could not read our conversation. 'Come on, let's get out of here. Let's go home.'

Her dear, puzzled face wrung my heart. It was enough to convince me to move. I pulled open the door, took a deep breath. If I did not go now, Abigail and Cutch would easily dissuade me. Copthorne and I had unfinished business, and if anything happened to Kate through my fault, I'd never be able to look myself in the eye again. The shouting at the front of the house was louder. I glanced at the window in an agony of indecision.

Wordlessly Cutch handed me his best sword, the one he'd got from Copthorne at Worcester.

'Thanks, you don't have to—'

'Come out alive, won't you?'

CHAPTER TWENTY-ONE

The Noose

Damn. The back door was locked and though Cutch had been able to squeeze his stringy shape through the pantry window, I knew my broad shoulders would never fit between the gap. I prowled the back of the house keeping close to the walls where it was blackest, and hearing all the time the shout, 'Devils out, devil's out!' waxing and waning, like waves breaking on a stormy beach. I stopped at the dining room at the back of the house. It had one window with wide enough mullions which would just about allow a man to pass through, but the glass was leaded in panes. I eyed it dubiously. It would take some smashing.

Even if I could get in that way, it would leave another access for Downall and his men. I weighed it up, but was too impatient to hesitate for long. It was the only way.

I waited for the chant to begin again to cover my noise, then smashed through with the pommel of my sword. Jagged diamonds of glass and lead stuck stubbornly to the window frame, but I ignored them and forced my way past, shielding my head with my doublet sleeves. My feet crunched on broken glass. I prayed nobody in the house had heard me.

Light spilled through the door from the hall, where the sconces must be lit. I crept towards it, sword at the ready, and tentatively pushing open the door, peered to my left. There was no sign of anyone as I crept down the corridor towards the drawing room. I didn't go in, in case Downall's mob saw me from the outside.

A scuff of footsteps above. So they were upstairs. Silently I trod up the shadowy staircase, step by step, my breath loud in my ears, fearing to hear a board creak and give me away. At the top of the stairs were two doors and I did not know which one to try.

'Drop your sword.'

I whipped round.

Copthorne's pistol was two feet from my chest. A large gash in his left shoulder had stained the velvet of his doublet with dark blood, and I could see the rip in the sleeve where my shot had hit him. He paid the wounds no attention. His expression was cold, neutral. Only his mouth betrayed a slight smile of satisfaction.

'Drop your sword,' he repeated.

We'll see about that, I thought. I lowered my weapon slowly to the ground, until I heard the thud of metal on board, then flinging myself upwards in one leap, I brought the sword sharply upwards to disarm him.

But he'd guessed my trick and was ready for me.

A blinding pain in the top of my head. Groaning, I fell sideways. My sword clattered to the ground. Through blurred eyes, I saw Copthorne examine the butt of his pistol, wipe it on his breeches.

My head throbbed so much I could hardly see.

He gestured through the door, 'Your friends are waiting inside. You will fight with us.' He put the pistol to my back and pushed me forwards.

Was it loaded? Not worth taking chances. I put my hand to my head, felt dampness there. Blood.

I staggered, grabbed hold of the door frame. It was slippery beneath my palm, but I clung on, nausea threatening to overwhelm me. The world was hazy. My sword. I'd left it downstairs.

Kate. Where was Kate?

My thoughts tumbled over each other trying to find a purchase.

Thomas's shadowed face appeared from behind the door. 'They're asking us to come out,' he said to Copthorne, a tremor in his voice. 'They'll break the door down. We should try and get ourselves away.'

'Coward.' Copthorne snapped from behind me. 'I'm the officer here. Now get back inside. You'll follow my orders.' A hard push and I cannoned into Thomas, and went sprawling on the floor, nose crunching down onto the floorboards.

When I looked up, it was to see the pale hem of Kate's dress, as she crouched next to me. Thank God, she was safe.

A deafening blast and Kate jumped back. Next to me a ragged hole in the floorboard smoked.

'Keep away from him,' Copthorne said.

I crawled to kneeling, 'Do as he says,' I begged her. Her eyes were wide with shock.

My legs felt like feathers, I could not stand up. There was nothing I could do in this state except bide my time, look for a chance to get her out of there.

Copthorne picked up a musket and thrust it at Thomas, then he thrust another to me, but I had no powder or shot to load it. 'Get to the window. Anyone tries the front door, or the windows, shoot.'

Thomas fumbled to take hold of the weapon. He was white-faced and disheveled. Shakily, he rammed the ball down his musket, and struck a flint.

'Go on,' urged Copthorne, pointing his pistol at him.

Thomas peered gingerly from the window, then pushed open the casement. A waft of night air.

'Fanshawe! Come out, or we'll come in and get you.' Downall's voice.

I stood up, grasping the wall for support, Kate ignored Copthorne's order to leave me, and propped me by the elbow. The room swung into focus. Think, man.

I gave Kate a look that I hoped was reassuring. 'Find me powder and shot,' I whispered.

'I'll not be driven from my own house,' Thomas called out of the window. 'Go home now. We can discuss everything peaceably in the morning.'

A murmur of dissent from the men outside. 'The Manor don't belong to you no more,' said another voice. 'It belongs to Parliament, and we're here to see they get it.'

Thomas hesitated, 'They're saying—'

'Are you for the King or not? Out of my way!' Copthorne strode over to the window, elbowed Thomas aside, wrenched the musket from his grasp, aimed and fired. Ignoring the smoke, he flung the weapon back at Thomas's feet. 'Re-load,' he said.

Outside, a woman started to scream.

He'd hit someone.

I staggered to the window, with my empty musket in my hand. Below us the lawns were massed with people. I blinked, my eyes struggling to focus, uncertain at what I was seeing.

There must have been a hundred people, more even, pressing in, forming a ragged circle around a body lying on the ground in front of the main door. A woman in a bright white coif crouched there over the splayed out figure on the drive. When she turned I recognised her straight away. Goodwife Soper.

'Fire! Or I'll shoot you dead.' Copthorne pressed his pistol to my back.

'It's empty,' I protested. 'I need powder and shot.'

Copthorne grabbed my gun, turned it on me and pulled the trigger.

When it didn't fire, he shoved me out of the way, fired his pistol into the crowd.

A sharp crack, and a roar from outside. I reeled away from the window. They'll lynch us, I thought. The war was not over after all, and we were on the front line of the battlefield. Immediately I heard the sound of splintering wood and breaking glass below.

Thomas took hold of Kate's hand, whispered, 'Quick, wife! The back stairs.'

I saw Kate snatch her hand away. She looked to me, her face full of questions.

'Go!' I mouthed.

Copthorne was reloading. He pointed the pistol at my chest, threw me powder and shot and told me to prime my musket. I obeyed, with one eye watching Kate.

She hesitated, eyes brim full of anguish.

'Come on!' hissed Thomas.

Still she hesitated. She shook her head at him.

'Don't be frightened, I—'

'No.' She cut him off. 'Everything I love is here.' She cast her eyes to me.

Thomas stiffened. His mouth twitched with unspoken words. Then he pulled back his shoulders as if to show he did not care, gave me a long hard stare. 'I see you've overstepped your duty, Chaplin. If I ever get out of here, I'll see you rot in hell.'

Downstairs, the noise of boots and the clang of iron in the front hall. Doors banging downstairs. Copthorne rushed to the window.

Thomas held out his hand one last time, but Kate lowered her eyes. Thomas shot me a look of hatred before he turned tail and ran.

I grabbed my chance. My knife hissed from its scabbard and I leapt up behind Copthorne, but he turned and the metal barrel of the pistol clashed against my knife. He tried to fire, but the barrel was empty.

I thrust the knife towards his throat, but it stopped a whisker shy of his skin. Was I going to turn into my father? I swallowed, unable to finish it.

Copthorne's eyes flared wide when the death blow did not come.

Shouts on the stairs, the clatter of boots.

'Lock the door,' I yelled to Kate.

'The rebels will kill you, if they get in,' I pressed my blade closer, 'I have no need to shed more Copthorne blood.'

'What do I care? My family died for the King. It would dishonour their memory if I did not fight,' he said. 'I swore I'd not wait for Heaven's justice. I'll not give in, not until the last of Cromwell's dogs has his teeth in the dust.'

'Ralph?' A wary voice from the corner. Kate. The single word conveyed a warning.

An enormous bang as something hit the door. Copthorne startled, but I held him tight to the wall.

'Too late,' I said, 'They're here. You should have taken your chance whilst you could.'

I saw something flicker in his eyes that could have been fear.

Kate whispered, 'Lord have Mercy.' She hurried to my side just as the door burst its lock and flew open. A crowd of men stormed in, manhandled it aside like driftwood.

There was no time to do anything before they were upon us. The smell of old hemp shirts, leather and drink. I grabbed Kate by the arm, but they lifted her bodily and despite my clinging, her hand slipped from my fingers. No! I tried to follow, but she was out of the door carried on a wave of shouting men.

My arms were grasped on each side. One man pulling one way and one the other. I thought my arms might leave their sockets.

'This way!' growled the man on my right.

They dragged me to one side, but I just had time to glance across the room. Copthorne was using his pistol to bludgeon anyone within reach, but a heavily moustached man wrenched it from him, slugged him on the head with the stock of it. The blow made my own head throb in recognition. Copthorne's eyes glazed over as they dragged him away ahead of me.

Thump, thump. His boots banged against the wooden stairs.

'We've got him!' My arms were pinioned by the two burly farm-workers, and others were pushing me down the stairwell in the dark. It was hard to see, the men were black moving silhouettes against the flickering light.

People made way for us, then fell in behind until we emerged into the yard in a great tide of people with us at the head of it. Over on the lawn there was still a knot of shadows surrounding the spread-eagled body of John Soper.

Before me, the crowd parted to show Copthorne, lying in a crumpled heap on the cobbles. The buttons on his waistcoat glinted dully. His pale jaw was slack. A dark bruise over one side of his face. He did not move. It was obvious he was dead.

I searched the mob frantically for Kate, but she was already pulling herself up to standing from where she had been thrown down. 'What means all this?' she shouted, her voice high and imperious.

My heart went out to her. She was still intent on being the Lady of the Manor. It was a brave attempt, but futile.

Downall stepped forwards, and the crowd waited expectantly. He had their attention, being the big bullying brute he was. 'Where is your husband?'

Kate lifted her chin. 'He ran away.'

Downall walked slowly up to her, grabbed her roughly by the hair. 'I won't ask again. Where is he?'

'Leave her alone,' I said. 'She tells true. He's gone. He took his horse and left.'

Downall turned to me, his eyes glittering with malice. 'You traitor. Royalist scum.' He turned to the crowd. 'Here's the man who broke Ned Soper's arm, and shot his father stone dead from that window.' He pointed back to the house. 'I say we hang him.'

The crowd were roused to fever pitch, they surged forward. 'Fetch a rope!' shouted someone.

'Bring the woman,' Downall said. 'She can watch.'

My legs wanted to run, but I was surrounded. I had no weapon but my knife and there were too many people for me to fight my way out. Downall was at the head of them leading the way, I heard him shout, 'the barn.'

A jab in the cheek. A punch in the stomach. My heart beating like it would jump from my chest. Stumbling. Hauled up again. Feet dragging through stubble. The doors opening to a cavern of blackness. The crowd pushing me in, under smoking torches and lanterns.

It took several attempts for Downall to lasso the rope over the beam. Once it was there the noose swung back and forth. The crowd fell silent.

The noose was a symbol. A thing of awe.

My stomach turned to water.

'If you do this, God will strike you down! You will have killed an innocent man, and the Lord will remember.' Kate's voice was high and clear. 'It was not this man who pushed Ned Soper from the cart, it was me. And it was not he who shot Ned's father. It was Copthorne, the cavalier who lies dead in the yard. I saw him do it with my own eyes.'

There was a hubbub as men whispered to each other, but the noise was cut short by Downall. 'Fetch that stool,' he shouted.

One of Downall's lackeys dragged the stool beneath the noose.

'Think what you do!' Kate begged. 'This man fought for Parliament with his father at Worcester. He buried his father not a week past. Do you not remember?' Her eyes caught two women standing near the front, 'Audrey! Susan, do you not remember me? It's Kate. From the Diggers.'

'Never!' Susan clapped her hand to her mouth. A fevered discussion.

'Tis her,' Margery said, 'She was at a Diggers meeting right here. T'was but a few weeks ago.'

The front row began to murmur, but I could not hear more, because I was dragged to the stool. Aiming a kick with my foot I managed to knock it aside, but I felt the weight of the noose drape round my shoulders, heavy as a yoke.

'Men to the rope! We'll haul him up.' Downall shouted.

Someone tried to tether my arms but I flailed them free. Enough men stood by the rope to lift me by the neck, I knew.

'Let me pray!' I shouted. 'Surely I have the right to clear my conscience with God?'

The men holding me paused, though one still kept hold of the noose, pressing it to my shoulders.

Could this dark crowd of angry faces really be the folk of my village? Men I'd learned my letters with, the boys who'd helped me net tiddlers in the river, or taught me to ride?

It was too dark to recognise anyone, but they must be there, the folk that knew me from a boy. And this barn, this was where I'd first fallen in love with Kate. Was I to die here?

To my horror my throat tightened and I felt tears prickle my eyelids.

Not now. I couldn't cry now. They'd think me less of a man.

In the distance thunder rumbled in a low growl.

I swallowed, looked up at the trusses of the roof, saw the weight of rope slung over the beam above my head. It brought me to my senses.

'Dear God, I don't know how I come to be here,' I called out, more to the assembled crowd than to my maker. I shook my head at one of the men holding my arms. 'Don't know how I got into this mess. Except by my own anger and foolishness, I suppose.' I turned to the other, 'I was always too quick of temper, even as a lad.'

'Get on with it.' Downall said, 'Pray if you're going to.'

'Aye, I was daft to pick a quarrel with Downall here. If it is your will I should die, then so be it. But it does seem mighty strange to survive the battlefield and then to die at the hands of those I was fighting for. I would like pray with my brothers, like I used to. Are there no men left like me, men who want to build a fairer world? Will you pray with me?'

Nobody moved. Just before me lay a spade, put down by one of the mob. With a wrench, I freed myself, grabbed hold of it and raised it above my head.

The men at my side snatched at my arms to restrain me.

'Take him!' Downall shouted.

'No! Don't you understand? This is what I believe in. I'm a farmer. Since when has a spade been a weapon we turn on each other?' I shouted, brandishing it overhead.

Downall pulled the spade from me and flung it down. Though I was strong, I could do nothing as he crushed my wrists behind me, bone on bone, and tugged a rough winding of twine around them. A sharp pull. I began to panic. Too tight. It will stop my blood. A clap of thunder. I had to make them understand.

I railed again, with no arms to gesture, 'There are men here who fight not with swords, not with firepowder, but with spades like that one, and the sweat of their brows. They want to graft something useful, something lasting, from our common earth. Winstanley's men, the Diggers. Are there any of you here? Barton? Whistler?'

Two figures in the front row looked to each other, shuffled. I pointed my gaze at them. 'Will you pray with me now, the way we used to?'

They were reluctant. But Kate stepped boldly forward, dragging two women I recognised as Susan and Margery with her. A small gaggle of other women followed.

'Shame on you men!' Susan called back to the menfolk. 'Would you deny the lad a prayer? Prayers can hurt no-one! Let God be a witness to what goes on here.'

At the back, men stood on tiptoe, craned their necks to see. There was a hush, as if we had invited God into the barn, and he was watching us.

The men looked to each other, discomfited. But the women stood like rocks, defiant before Downall and his men. The rope chafed against my neck, my chest felt like it had already been cut open.

If these words were to be my last they had better be sincere. I thought of my mother and William, how much I loved them, yes, and even my father. Love for them all pierced my heart. If I should need to join them, then at least there would be a welcome for me.

I stood tall, calmed my breath. I looked straight to Kate, hoped my eyes would tell her what I could not openly say. Of all of them, I loved her best. I dropped my voice to a whisper.

'May God help you make of the Earth a common treasury for all, both rich and poor, that every one that is born in the land, may be fed equally by the Earth his mother that brought him forth, according to law of Creation.'

Kate held my gaze. 'Amen to that. And we pray that no man shall have dominion over another—'

'Enough!' Downall stepped forward in front of me. 'Are we going to let this gaggle of women prevent justice being done?'

'Don't seem much like justice to me,' came a muttered male voice.

From the massed men came whispers, 'He's right. I'm sick of all this strife,' and 'What are we fighting? She can't do much, little Katherine Fanshawe, not with no husband by her.' The man standing next to me with his hand on the noose stepped aside, held up his hands in a gesture of surrender.

'I'll not be party to this,' he said. 'If Chaplin's done something wrong there should be a trial. We should fetch Mallinson. Do it legal.'

'But he killed John Soper,' Downall said, 'and—'

'She said not,' Audrey said gesturing to Kate.

'Aye,' Susan said. 'She said that other man did it. Will you hang her too?'

'If need be! She's a Royalist,' Downall said. 'What's the matter with you all? You on the rope, pull!'

I squeezed my eyes shut, held my breath. Pray God make it quick. On the slate roof of the barn a sudden shiver of rain, a noise like lead shot rattling in a flask.

'I'll do it myself,' Downall's voice was almost drowned by the downpour.

I opened my eyes. 'No,' Barton shouted, barring his way. 'It don't seem right. I don't like rough justice. Let the law decide it.'

'Chaplin makes more sense than you do, Downall,' the man on the other side of me said, 'You do nothing but stir up shit. Have done since you were small.' He lifted the noose back over my head. I gasped for breath, even though it had never choked me.

I did not move. I stood there with everyone staring at me, feeling naked without that noose, like a newborn child.

By my foot a trickle of rain leaked through the roof into a dark stain. The man at my side took a knife and sawed through the bonds at my wrists. I turned to him, held out my hand. He shook it, grinning like a fool. I recognised my old schoolmaster, Mr Trimble. Tears were in both our eyes.

The crowd let out an audible sigh, then erupted into chatter. Barton and Whistler hurried up to me. 'Ralph,' Barton said, 'I didn't recognise you.'

'It's all right,' I said, colluding with his lie, 'it was dark.'

'Wait,' called Downall, but the villagers had turned back, quietened, like tired dogs after a day's hunting. Hats were being replaced on heads. Nobody looked at Downall. It was as if he didn't exist.

CHAPTER TWENTY-TWO

A Life, a Death

There was a crush to get out of the barn, with so many people, all trying to hold their aprons or their arms over their heads against the rain. I kept my hand on the small of Kate's back. The rain stung the cut on my head, but the pain was nothing in comparison to the elation I felt. We paused as the dwindling torches went ahead of us through the door, and the knots of people disappeared into the dark and the rain. Barton and Whistler hurried with us, with their wives and the other Digger women.

Nobody spoke, our heads were lowered against the weather. As we got to the yard I thought I heard the ring of hoofbeats in the distance. Automatically I pulled Kate back against the stable wall. 'What?' she said, her hair already glistening with beads of water

'Horses.'

Her eyes filled with fear. We watched the riders emerge from the dark fields and clatter into the yard. Six men with the glint of arms at their belts.

'Halt! Who goes there?' I called.

'Jacob Mallinson and the Constable's men. Your name, sir?' I did not answer, uncertain whether Jacob would give me a civil reception.

'It's us, Jacob. Seth Barton and Owen Whistler,' Barton said, 'on our way home.'

Jacob reined in his horse. 'What's gone on here? Abigail came with Cutch, to tell us there was trouble at the Fanshawes, but we couldn't understand it; she was too upset. I came straight over. My father follows in an evil temper, he is barely fit enough to ride. Where's Jack Downall?'

'I don't know. He went that way.' Whistler pointed.

'I need to speak to him, Father says we've to bring him to the lock-up, let him cool off. What about the Fanshawes? Are they within?'

Kate stepped forward. 'My husband has fled. There is only me.'

Jacob climbed down and spoke to the men behind him. 'Go and see if you can find Downall, or better still, Ralph Chaplin. Word is, they're the cause of it. I'll go with Mistress Fanshawe and check the house.'

'Aye,' said one of his men, wiping his face of water, 'They're all still coming up from the barn, I'll try there.' They wheeled their horses and galloped away.

'Kate,' Jacob said, his voice full of concern, 'Are you alright? Where's Ralph?'

'Here,' I said, stepping out from under the dripping eaves.

It was time to face it all.

Jacob squinted at me through the rain. My appearance seemed to rouse his anger. 'What's going on? I met Goodwife Soper on the road. She says Soper's dead, and that it was you that shot him.'

'Not true,' Kate says.

'Hellfire, Ralph! You're always responsible, wherever trouble is. Father's men will arrest you if they see you. What in God's name are you doing here?'

'I can't run any longer. I came to find the man who killed my mother and my brother.'

Jacob's face set hard like a stone. Rain poured off his hat in a steady stream.

'Is this a joke?' he said.

'No, I swear. I haven't told Abigail yet, but Mother is dead, and William...' My voice cracked. I shut my lips, looked down, tried to gather myself.

How could anyone do that? To a helpless woman and a baby? But then I remembered what Cutch had told me about Father. Even now it did not seem possible. Nothing seemed real.

Jacob caught the look on my face. 'Jesus.' He was silent a moment, taking it in. 'Ralph, where's Martha?' He took my collar, shook me from my thoughts.

'No, it's all right. She's safe. I took her to the vicarage.'

'Quick. Come in the house,' Kate said, against the driving rain. 'We can't talk here.' We ran for the shelter of the house, heads down, feet splashing up wet from the slippery cobbles. As we arrived at the front door, three ragged black crows flew silently into the dark.

In the house we sat round the kitchen table. My elbows dripped onto the wood. It was a while before anyone spoke. 'Do you think Downall will come back?' Kate asked.

'My father and his men will round him up, but they may yet come here to get an account from you, of what's happened.' Jacob said.

'I hope not. I can't face it,' Kate said.

She stood and went to the door, drew the bolt across to bar it, but she did not sit. Her face was white. Tendrils of hair hung wetly round her face. She came and put a hand on my shoulder. 'What happened to your mother, Ralph?'

'Copthorne. Revenge. My father massacred his family.'

'I'd no idea. When he arrived, Copthorne told Thomas he was a friend of his uncle. Said he was passing through on his way to London to get a boat to France. I thought it was odd he had no retinue, but we had no reason not to believe him. He knew friends of my uncle, and Thomas was glad to see a fellow cavalier. Thank heaven you came.'

'What happened to him?' Jacob asked.

'Dead. Downall's men got him. The last I saw of him he'd been bludgeoned down in the yard and—'

A creak of a floorboard above.

We froze. Silence.

Jacob stood quietly and drew his sword.

'Wait here,' I said to Kate.

I followed Jacob as he crept up the stairs. My blood was all a-jangle, my eyes staring round in the darkness. We crept across the corridor until we came to the upstairs chamber with the smashed door.

Empty.

Another creak of a board from the next room. Jacob pushed the door open with the tip of his finger.

A sudden flurry of movement from behind the draped bed. 'Look out!' I yelled. Jacob shot backwards. A dark figure swayed before the moonlight pooling through the window.

The silhouette was unmistakeable. Copthorne. But I thought he was dead. What was he? Invincible? His sword was already out, shining silver in the gloom. I recognised it as the one Cutch had given me, the one from Worcester.

Jacob turned just in time, went for his musket, but there was no time to deal with powder and shot, even if it had been dry enough.

Realising, Jacob took a step backwards, shocked, drew his sword. 'Put your weapon down,' he called, 'in the name of the Law.'

Copthorne's answer was to hurtle forward and make a slash at Jacob's chest. Jacob leapt to the side on instinct, but Copthorne ignored him. He was coming for me.

I was unarmed, had nothing to protect me. Copthorne made a thrust, but I dodged, held my hands up. 'I don't want to fight,' I shouted, as I retreated. 'I'm sorry. We're even now. We don't need more blood.'

'Coward.' Copthorne shouted, advancing.

He was haggard, his hair bedraggled and one eye half-closed from a blow to the face. I backed away towards the door.

'Here!' Jacob threw his sword to me and I reached out to catch its glinting arc without thinking. But I did not want to fight.

Copthorne goaded me with the tip of his sword, waiting for my anger to rise, his blade circling mine with dips and flashes.

'No,' I said. I knew now how precious life was. 'My father shed enough Copthorne blood. I will not become him. It stops here.'

His answer was a grunt and another thrust. Jesus. I parried it but did not counter with a strike. I saw the whites of his eyes disappear in anger and he let out a roar, pressed a series of vicious upper-cuts towards my stomach and chest. Though I could barely see them in the dark, I parried them, my breath coming in short sharp puffs. Now I was backed against the wall, my sword held in front like a standard. I blocked a blow to the temple from the pommel of the sword that almost broke my knuckles and I winced and gave an involuntary shiver of pain.

I heard Jacob cry a warning, and saw him bring down the butt of his musket on Copthorne's head. But Copthorne did not flinch, the bloodlust darkened his face, as he made one thrust after another.

Side. Shift. Side. Block. I was tiring. Legs shaking. Be strong, don't fight back. His sword kept coming. Over his shoulder I caught a glimpse of something.

Father? A pale figure, younger than I remembered, wearing his familiar slouched-brim hat.

The world turned slower, the noise of the clashing swords stilled. I blinked. Father was gone. The noise was suddenly loud in my ears. The door to the side of me opened, and I turned as Kate came in.

The first thrust to my chest did not register. You've torn my doublet, I thought.

But my arms felt weaker, like arms of straw.

Kate? Was she real? The woman entering the room was grainy, indistinct. My heart seemed to fly out to her.

The second thrust winded me, slammed my back to the wall. I saw Jacob's mouth open in a cry but could not hear it. I knew I was sliding down the wall, the plasterwork scraped down my back, but it felt comfortable, restful. I saw the third thrust coming, but found myself ready to welcome it, like a blessing. The tip of the sword was beautiful, the gleaming edge anointed with red blood. I sighed as it entered my chest, but felt no pain.

Copthorne stepped back, satisfied. The sword slid out of my chest. His arms hung limply, and a bead of blood dripped from the point of his blade into my open palm. He stared down at me, but...

Up. There I was, lying on the ground. Head tilted awkwardly against the wainscot. A bloom of something dark spreading over my chest. Outrage swelled in my chest but scattered out like powder.

What was happening? I shouted to Jacob, but he ignored me, he was crouching over the slumped figure, feeling at the neck.

'Do something!' Kate shouted.

Jacob shook his head.

'I'm here.' I tried to reach Kate, but she was bending over the body on the floor.

'Ralph!' she cried, 'Ralph, my love, talk to me. Don't leave me.'

'No! I'm here!' I tried to touch her, but my hand flew through space. I could not gather myself together. I was all whiteness and nothingness.

A hammering on the front door.

With a thump I was back inside my body. I groaned, began to tremble. I was cold as ice.

Jacob rushed to the window. 'It's my father,' he said, 'and reinforcements.'

Copthorne staggered past us out of the room.

'Stop him!' Kate cried. I tried to hold her words somehow, but they drifted from me. I could not move. The world was coming and going.

'Ralph,' Kate said, 'hold on. You've got to hold on.' She put her warm fingers on my forehead, brushed away the hair. Tears fell onto my cheeks. 'You'll be fine,' she said, trembling fingers pulling my shirt over the wounds. 'We'll build that Diggers dream right here at Markyate.'

My breath rasped shallower now. No energy to breathe. Must tell her. Tell her what? My mind could not get a purchase.

Kate began to sing the familiar song, so low and sweet; it hurt me to hear it,

> 'You noble Diggers all,
> Stand up now, stand up now,
> You noble Diggers all, stand up now.
>
> The good land to maintain,
> seeing Cavaliers by name
> Your digging doth disdain
> Stand up now, stand up now, Diggers all.
>
> Your houses they pull down,
> stand up now, stand up now,
> Your houses they pull down, stand up now...'

Kate's voice broke, she pressed her lips to mine, but somehow mine would not move to kiss her back. Her voice quavered back to life, defiant now.

'But the gentry must come down and the poor shall wear the crown...'

'Stand up now, Diggers all.' I whispered, but the words did not come. 'I love you Kate. I'll never leave you, I promise.'

Her deep green eyes held mine. 'Dearest heart,' she said. But suddenly I was flying away from her, like a petal blown in the wind. I fought to go back, but there was not enough substance left of me. Just such love and longing that my whole body seemed to glow with it.

'Ralph!' Kate was shaking the person on the ground.

Tell her it's all right! Sit up, damn you.

But I could do nothing.

I tried to go towards her, but a voice calling my name stopped me. I turned. It was Mother, with William in her arms. A great rush of emotion blew me into pieces.

Her image wavered, flickered, but she smiled. My thought was clear as a spring. 'I thought you were...'

She nodded. She had read my thought.

'Am I..?'

Her answer ignored my question. 'Go after Copthorne,' she seemed to say, 'finish the story. I'll watch over Kate whilst you go.'

I felt myself attached to Kate, with a thread as strong as steel, but part of me wanted to move, to fly free in this new free body I had become. With a spurt of will-power, I gathered myself. With a rush, and hardly meaning to move, I was outside looking down on the highway.

CHAPTER TWENTY-THREE

Retribution

Along the road Copthorne galloped, on his big black beast, like a streak of sorrow. And after him, Jacob and his father and the constable's men, pounding through the rain. Over the bridge across the swollen river, over the county boundary, they pursued him.

Jacob's horse grew tired and wanted to slow, but he urged it on. Steam rose from the horses' flanks, foam flecked their necks, but Copthorne's horse turned into the woods and pelted down the bridleways as if it had quicklime on its heels. At length they came to a wide expanse of grass with scarcely a tree in sight. There was nowhere Copthorne could hide.

On the other side of the common, the edge of the forest beckoned. I saw him throw a sharp glance behind, and on seeing the party of six men gaining on him, clap his spurs to his horse's flank and forge onwards the woods. If he got there he would soon lose them, I knew.

The thought came to me, if I was dead, I could not die.

I drew together, concentrating myself into a small point of intent, then flew like a hawk round the black beast's ears. The horse sensed me. It threw back its head and shrieked, reared on its hind legs, hooves thrumming the air. But the iron shoes passed right through me, all I felt was a frisson, a metallic tingle. Copthorne grew angry, flapped his reins to push his horse on, but it trod on the spot, wild-eyes staring at me, despite his curses.

Copthorne threw himself down and ran for the cover of the trees. I kept pace with him easily, gliding over the wet grass as he tripped and stumbled. I could smell his fear – a fetid odour like a fox on heat. His horse gave a shrill whinny and bolted back along the clear common.

The drumming of hooves grew closer, and made me slip quick as a will o' the wisp into the trees. Next time I looked they were almost upon him, but Copthorne kept on running, right in the path of the horses, his breath panting fast in his throat.

A thump and he was down, caught in the legs of Jacob's horse. The crack of a bone, the clank of a scabbard as it hit the ground. The soft suck of horses' hooves in mud and flesh. The men jumped from their mounts and bodily pressed Copthorne's flailing arms into the earth. They kept him there, groaning, face squashed into the mud.

He looked small, and pale and younger than I remembered, for I felt both old and young together. His face was a mass of gashes, his body battered and bleeding.

The air bristled, the horses sidled uneasily.

A rush of affection for Jacob, so serious-faced, so solid, holding Copthorne down, but gently, so as not to hurt him too much.

After a few more minutes another party of horsemen arrived, riding slower.

'It's Father,' Jacob said, to his companions.

Constable Mallinson looked down from atop his horse. His left arm was still in a sling. He stared down at the broken body of Copthorne. Jacob let him go, and he rolled over, gasping for breath.

'You'll hang,' Constable Mallinson said to him.

I remembered the feeling of the rope on my neck and wanted to cry, but I had no eyes to do so. Another wasted life. How foolish men were.

My sadness swelled like a storm cloud. It made me want to move, to swirl like a tornado. I shot off into the woods to weave between the trees. Overhead the crows flew up from their roosts with indignant cries, their black, glittering eyes fixed on Copthorne.

CHAPTER TWENTY-FOUR

The Wake

The autumn rain had softened the ground. Cutch and Jacob helped the sexton dig graves for my corpse, for those of my mother and for poor William, whilst Barton and the other Diggers had dug with Ned Soper for his father.

Now Abigail and Kate stood under the trees at the edge of the churchyard arm in arm, red-eyed and silent waiting for the coffins to arrive. Most of the villagers were there, a respectfully quiet crowd, with long grey faces and curious eyes. So many deaths in one week, it had sobered them all.

You want to know if love survives death? Well I can tell you that it does. I have never felt such a love as on that day, watching my Kate draw herself up in church and address the congregation. Her face was pale but determined, her copper hair a splash of fire against her sombre gown. She held herself like a queen.

'I make you all a solemn promise,' she said, 'That whilst I am able, I will offer every man a strip of land to till if he wants it. That as far as possible we shall live by our own hard work. Jacob Mallinson has agreed to oversee it, with the help of his father. Those who fought for the right to their own future shall have it.'

'What does your husband say?' Ned Soper's snide voice came from the back, hastily hushed by the women beside him.

'He says nothing,' retorted Kate. 'He has fled to France, and until he returns, the future is in your own hands. You can work with me or against me. We have seen what war does to those we love. Let's have no more of it.'

As she spoke I felt her think of me. A sudden shaft of light, as though I had flared momentarily brighter. And my love expanded in response, a spark shooting into flame. It was the feeling I had when I looked into her eyes, a love so intense it was pure pain.

Kate was moving down the church, the whisper of her skirts soft against the flagstones. I reached out to her, but my hands were like smoke, too weak to catch her. Her thoughts turned instead to Abi who was waiting for her, head bowed in grief in the family pew. The first vestige of unease trembled through me.

What if they forgot me?

I saw Kate squeeze Abi's hand to give her comfort, felt Abi's sad memories of me run through my body like a fish through water.

'Why didn't he fight?' Abigail asked her.

'Because he had conquered himself. It was the bravest thing I ever saw.'

After the service and the burial Kate and Abi set off to walk back to the Manor together, accompanied by Jacob and my old friend Cutch. How sturdy he looked now, when I had thought him quite scrawny next to my well-muscled frame.

My sister Elizabeth ran to catch up with them, her blue silk ribbons trailing from her bonnet in the breeze. Cutch smiled warmly at her, but her eyes were only on Jacob. She pressed her way between Jacob and Abi and started to talk animatedly, flashing her arching eyes at Jacob, about what sort of food Mistress Binch might have provided for the wake.

I wanted to reprimand her, tell her to leave well alone, but I could do nothing. I buzzed like a fly round her head, hoping to give her a headache at least.

It was then that I saw them.

Just behind the stand of yew trees near the lych gate,

the solid outline of Jack Downall and a man in a sober well-cut doublet and wide-crowned hat. Mallinson had told Downall to leave the county, find work elsewhere. Something about the way he was hiding in the trees was not right.

The two men were talking low and quiet. They shook hands and Downall went across the fields away from the church and the rest of the congregation. A slight smile warmed his usually sullen features. I flew over to follow the other man to see who he might be. It was then I saw he was limping, an uneven gait that reminded me...

Grice. The old overseer of the estate that had been sacked by the Fanshawes. His pinched face was unmistakable.

It gave me a jolt that scattered me. What was he doing here? I hadn't seen him since Abigail and I left him tied up in the forest waiting for the Royalists to finish him. His presence was a bad omen. I followed him, close to his neck, seeing the strands of greying hair straggle from beneath his hat, the dark line of stubble at his jaw.

He shivered and turned a moment, looked down the path behind him. His eyes were calculating and sharp. At first I thought he'd seen me, but then his gaze shifted from side to side and he whipped his head back to the front.

A carriage stood idling for him by the lych gate and he heaved himself in, gripping the doors with bony white hands. His wooden boot banged against the running plate, and he dragged it inside. Moments later the carriage bowled away in the direction of Wheathamstead.

What was he doing here, talking to Downall?

I must tell Kate.

But Kate and Abi were walking companionably towards the Manor, oblivious.

I tried to get their attention. Kate! Abi! I cried out with all of my being.

Kate stopped, I felt her think of me. She turned to look behind. *Ralph?* But Jacob took her arm, smiled in sympathy and led her on.

No! Please, you have to hear me! Grice was here. Please someone, listen.

But nobody heard me. I had vowed to Kate I would never leave her, that no matter what, I would always be there to protect her. But what use was I now? I called and called, until I was too disintegrated to muster myself.

I ached then in frustration, for the body I had lost. For the dear sweet feeling of the ground underfoot, for a mouth to speak, and hands to touch, and a heart to beat faster when Kate looked my way. It was agony to see Kate and Abigail turn into the big stone gates, not knowing that Downall and Grice had been here in Markyate, just out of their sight.

If I was going to make them hear me, I'd need practice, I realised. I'd need people to think of me too, to keep me strong. When people remember me I grow brighter, my body becomes a pale mist like a shadow in reverse. But when I'm absent from people's minds I become so transparent I'm imperceptible.

I swooped down the driveway after them in a stream of vapour and intent.

CHAPTER TWENTY-FIVE

Restless Spirit

Although the door to the Manor House was locked, I entered through the crack under the door, and found them in the bed chamber. Abigail had untied Kate's back lacing and was loosening her bodice, but Kate told her she could manage and bade her go. Abigail kissed her cheek fondly and picked up her night light. As soon as she'd gone, Kate slumped onto the bed, face white with exhaustion. Funeral feasts are long affairs and I knew she'd played the role of hostess without thought for herself. Now she lay on her side on top of the covers, too limp to move.

After a few moments she sat, slipped off her bodice to reveal her chemise. She thought she was alone in her chamber, and guiltily I realised I might see more than she wished me to see. Should I go? The air around me where my body once was, still ached for her touch. I'd thought of it so often, our fevered coupling on the flagstone floor, and last week I would have been hungry to see another glimpse of her naked skin, but now? Would it have any meaning for me now, in my changed state?

She pulled her chemise over her head, and I saw the swell of her breasts above it.

Oh yes, it still had meaning. The sight turned me all a-tingle, as if I might even be able to make myself more solid, more tangible. Kate paused with the chemise bunched in her hand. Her thoughts of me swirled around the room like whirlpools, but their movement gave me renewed strength.

'Kate?' I called.

She turned slowly, eyes alert, wide, scanning the room.

'Ralph?' Her voice was a whisper as she strained to see me.

'I'm here.' I sent the thought with all my might.

Her hand reached out into empty air.

I conjured the image of Downall and Grice, just as I had seen them, by the lych gate. I squeezed the detail from the scene, the slub-weave of Downall's fox-coloured jerkin, the way Grice's hat shadowed his face right down to the stubbled jaw, hoping to make the picture sharp.

Kate stood up and paced the room, anxiety creasing her white face. 'Ralph? Are you there?'

Yes! I pushed my presence into the silence.

She paused, held her breath. Her thoughts said, 'I feel it. I can feel the danger, but what should I do?'

Was she talking to me?

I had no answer. The room fell into a pregnant silence again.

'Ralph, if you're there, then give me a sign,' she said.

What could I do? I summoned my strength, moved over to the candle on the mantel. I'd flicker the flame, even snuff it out. At least I could try. With a supreme effort I plummeted towards the flame.

A crash and the room plunged into darkness. I heard Kate's sharp intake of breath.

God's truth, I'd done it! I was stronger than I thought, the whole candlestick had tumbled to the ground. My elation was short-lived; my energy was spent, fading.

The sound of running feet.

The door burst open and the light from the hall sconces flickered into the room.

'What is it?' Abigail rushed in, 'Something fell. I felt the vibration of it.'

Kate's face was blank with shock. 'Ralph. He was here, I swear it.'

Abigail put her arm around her shoulders. 'Don't. I know it's hard, but he's gone. He's not coming back.'

'He knocked the candle off the mantel.'

Abigail stooped to pick up the candlestick, jammed the nub of wax back in its holder, lit the wick and set the light back on the mantelpiece. Sighing, she shut the casement window with a bang. 'Only the wind,' she said.

'He was here, I know it.' Kate said, grasping her by the wrist.

'It's been a long day,' Abigail said, 'and it will feel longer tomorrow. Try to sleep.'

Kate's face was troubled and uncertain, but Abigail patted her on the arm and withdrew. As soon as she'd gone, Kate came to the candlestick and weighed it in her hands, unfastened the latch and pushed the window open.

The slight breeze ruffling the trees made the candle flame dance and waver, but it did not blow out. Not even when she held it outside at arm's length.

'He was here,' she murmured, 'I swear it. Either that, or grief makes me lose my wits.'

They hanged Copthorne on Finchley Common. The sight of his feet dangling off the ground gave me no pain. He seemed to brush through me as his spirit went, not wanting to tarry. Not like me, tied here somehow by love.

I heard someone in the crowd ask who he was. 'Chaplin, the highwayman,' the woman answered.

'You're wrong,' I thought. But so a legend was born, that I was hanged on Finchley Common. Copthorne, Chaplin, what did she care? It was an easy mistake to make. And in truth, it is good to be spoken of. I burn brighter then. The living fear to die, but the dead fear to be forgotten.

So I must tell this story, and keep on telling it, because it is the only way I can summon the strength I need to help Kate, to keep her there - where her feet can touch the good sweet earth, her hair blow in the wind, as she looks out over the land she loves. I am more use to her dead than I ever was alive. I am her inspiration to build the future.

Historical Notes from the Author

Ghosts in the Seventeenth Century

The belief that people might manifest themselves as spirits after their death was widespread during the seventeenth century. It was part of a religious world view that accepted other magical creatures, including witches, fairies, elves, brownies and hobgoblins.

Catholics believed in Purgatory, a place between Heaven and Hell, where the person could repent of their wrong-doings, and then move up to Heaven or, if not, downwards to Hell. This limbo was where ghosts resided, caught between the living world and their ultimate destination. But with the Reformation, belief in Purgatory disappeared and instead souls were judged almost immediately and were sent down to eternal flames or up to salvation.

However, belief in ghosts could not be squashed in Protestant England. After all, people argued, the Bible has ghostly appearances such as Samuel to Saul (Samuel 1:28) and Moses and Elias seeing Christ (Mark 9:4), and doesn't this suggest that God believes ghosts exist?

However, because few believed in Purgatory any more, the concept of what a ghost might be, was forced to change. By the middle of the seventeenth century, returning spirits were believed to be driven by personal need, rather than simply because they had not yet found their final destination. In the literature of the time, when ghosts appeared, it was usually to effect a change in our world.

In Shakespeare's *Hamlet*, the ghost urges Hamlet to take revenge. Ghosts often appeared to right a wrong, or to frighten a guilty party into putting things right. And this view is still common today.

Evidence of ghosts appears in the seventeenth century printed pamphlets, and figured prominently in traditional British folk songs.

Examples from the seventeenth century are *Sweet William's Ghost*, *The Wife of Usher's Well*, and *The Unquiet Grave*, all of which speak of dead lovers or children who return.

> *The twelvemonth and a day being up,*
> *The dead began to speak:*
> *"Oh who sits weeping on my grave,*
> *And will not let me sleep?"*
>
> *"'T is I, my love, sits on your grave,*
> *And will not let you sleep;*
> *For I crave one kiss of your clay-cold lips,*
> *And that is all I seek."*

"You crave one kiss of my clay-cold lips,
But my breath smells earthy strong;
If you have one kiss of my clay-cold lips,
Your time will not be long.

The Unquiet Grave

Ghosts might also give warnings or prophecies. Keith Thomas, in his book *Religion and the Decline of Magic* (1971), quotes examples of ghosts revealing the location of money or of crucial documents relating to property, especially after the turmoil of the English Civil War.

It was widely believed that spirits travelled in straight lines, and so could be trapped by labyrinths or mazes, and confused by crossroads. They also could not pass through water so, to prevent the deceased returning to haunt their old dwelling, holy water could be sprinkled in a circle around it. Superstition also led to corpses being carried with their feet facing away from the direction of their home so that they would not return.

Over the years many claim to have witnessed wisps of light or blue flames dancing along the old coffin routes to the village church, or hovering in burial grounds. When they appear they are said to foretell a death.

A well-known seventeenth century ghost associated with the Fanshawe family was the red-haired banshee who haunted the O'Briens of Rossmore in Ireland. She appeared at the bedroom window of Lady Ann Fanshawe, Kate's aunt and, according to her diary, the spectre kept her awake all night with her terrible weeping, only disappearing at sunrise.

In the legend of The Wicked Lady, (see below) there are many sightings of Katherine Fanshawe (Kate) after her death, although most of these date from the Victorian era. Ralph Chaplin dies early on in the legend of The Wicked Lady, but I felt that his viewpoint was an important one and so I made the decision to write this book from the point of view of his ghost. His continuing influence and love for Kate can be felt in the third book of the trilogy, 'Lady of the Highway', (to follow in 2016), which tells Katherine Fanshawe's story after Ralph's death, and of course features Abigail too.

The Real Lady Katherine Fanshawe and Ralph Chaplin

Lady Katherine Fanshawe really did exist. Katherine was born on 4th May 1634 into a wealthy family, the Ferrers. Tragically, her father, Knighton Ferrers, died two weeks before she was born, and her grandfather shortly after, leaving her the sole heir to a fortune.

A few years later her mother was married again, to the spendthrift and gambler Sir Simon Fanshawe. Unfortunately, Katherine's mother died when she was only eight, leaving her at the mercy of the Fanshawe family. Sir Simon supported the Royalist cause and the King needed money to fund his army. Sir Simon conceived of a plan to marry off his nephew, Thomas Fanshawe, to the rich heiress, thus gaining control over Katherine's wealth and land.

During much of the English Civil War Katherine's uncle and husband were away fighting, and spent much of the latter part of the war in exile in France. Whilst researching this trilogy, the stories about Lady Katherine that I found really fascinating were the reports of her exploits as a notorious highwaywoman. What went on during her husband's absence that would lead her to do the things she did? I decided there must be a long history behind her legend as 'The Wicked Lady', and that the answer could not be as simplistic as a lust for excitement.

There are no historical records about Ralph Chaplin, although his name always appears in the stories. He is widely believed to have been Lady Katherine's lover, and to have been a farmer's son. Other than that, little is known of him, and I could find no archival records for his existence. That being the case, I have taken the liberty of giving him a fictional family, including a deaf sister called Abigail. Whilst researching this book about Ralph Chaplin I took into account both the real history of the events of the English Civil War, and the legend of The Wicked Lady which features his lover, Kate. I also discovered that Lady Ann Fanshawe, Kate's aunt, wrote a diary, and I used this valuable insight into the period as part of my research.

Lady Katherine Fanshawe, (Kate), Ralph Chaplin and his sister Abigail also appear in my earlier book, 'Shadow on the Highway,' which tells Abigail's story. Look out for 'Lady of the Highway', the culmination of the trilogy, which tells Lady Katherine's (Kate's) story.

Roundheads and Cavaliers

This book is set at the very end of the English Civil War. Ralph takes part in the Battle of Worcester, fighting for Parliament, (the Roundheads) against the Cavaliers of the King's Army.

In the middle of the seventeenth century, England went to war – not with another country, but with itself. This was a war which came and went, with brief periods of peace between each bout of fighting. It spread to Scotland, Wales and Ireland and to all levels of society. The dispute was one in which both men and women were prepared to take sides on matters of principle, and fight for their beliefs to the death.

In simple terms, the War was one between the King and his followers – the King's Army, and Parliament on the other – The New Model Army, led by Cromwell. Sometimes these groups are known as Cavaliers and Roundheads. 'Cavalier' from the Spanish, *caballero*, originally meant a mounted soldier, but came to be used as an insult to denote someone who would put themselves above their station. 'Roundhead' was a term used to describe the short-haired apprentices who first came out in favour of Parliament.

The fighting was over matters of political policy, and on how Britain should be governed. The differences between the two factions were complicated by their opposing religious views; the Anglicanism of the King versus the Puritanism of Cromwell's men. The War began when the port of Hull refused to open its gates to the King, and in 1642 the King proclaimed war on his rebellious subjects.

The English Civil War killed about two hundred thousand people, almost four percent of the population, and brought disease and famine in its wake. It divided families and stripped the land of food and wealth, as troops rampaged the countryside foraging and plundering whatever they could find.

Towns were flattened, and communities dispersed. For example, records show that Parliamentary troops blew up more than two hundred houses at Leicester just to provide a clear line of fire, whilst four hundred more were destroyed at Worcester and another two hundred at Faringdon.

There were nearly ten years of fighting and unrest. Some children barely knew their fathers as they had been away in the wars for most of that time. In effect there were three main periods of fighting, and this book is set right at the end, when the King is finally routed by Cromwell's increasingly efficient New Model Army.

The seventeenth century saw a King executed, followed by the establishment of a military dictatorship under Cromwell. It was also a time that transformed society, and gave birth to new ideas about political and religious liberty, as demonstrated by the Diggers and sundry other sects with alternative or utopian ideals.

The Diggers

The Diggers were the first group of people to try and live in what we would nowadays call a 'commune.'

Led by Gerrard Winstanley, the movement began in Cobham, England, in 1649, but rapidly spread to other parishes in the southern area of England.

The name 'The Diggers' came from Winstanley's belief that the earth was made to be 'a common treasury for all', and that all should be able to dig it, and provide themselves with what was necessary for human survival – food, warmth and shelter. The Diggers consisted mostly of poorer families that had no land of their own. They took over common land which was not already used, and began to cultivate it. They did not believe in enclosing the land, or separating one part of the earth from another.

Rich land-owners found these ideas threatening, and organised men to destroy the Diggers homes and ruin their crops in an effort to drive them off the land. The Diggers made several unsuccessful attempts to build houses in different locations, but were suppressed by the land-owning classes and dispersed by force, and the communities wiped out.

Although the Diggers were a short-lived movement, their ideas had a far-reaching effect, sowing the seeds of communal living and self-sufficiency for future generations. There is still a Diggers Festival every year in Wigan in England, where Winstanley was born.

Acknowledgements

Thank you to Peter, James, Fiona, Robert, Karen, Claire, John and Jenny who were my early test readers.

I read many books, pamphlets and archive material on the period, but I am grateful to the following books which formed the bedrock of my research:

By The Sword Divided – John Adair
The English Civil Wars – Maurice Ashley
Going to the Wars – Charles Carlton
The English Civil War at First Hand – Tristram Hunt

Thank you for choosing to purchase 'Spirit of the Highway'. If you have enjoyed it, please consider writing a review or recommending it to a friend.

If you have any queries about the book or this series, I am always happy to chat to readers. You can find me on Twitter @swiftstory, or on my website www.deborahswift.com

Made in the USA
Charleston, SC
24 November 2015